the Lost Summer

KATHRYN WILLIAMS

DISNEY • HYPERION BOOKS

New York

Printed in the United States of America
First Edition
1 3 5 7 9 10 8 6 4 2

Library of Congress Cataloging-in-Publication Data on file.
ISBN 978-1-4231-0128-4
Reinforced binding
Designed by Roberta Pressel
Visit www.hyperionteens.com

SUSTAINABLE FORESTRY INITIATIVE

Certified Fiber Sourcing

www.sfiprogram.org

THIS LABEL APPLIES TO TEXT STOCK

For Novella Thérèse Adams

Day is done, gone the sun
From the hills, from the lake,
from the sky.
All is well; safely rest.
God is nigh.

— "Taps"

Prologue

I died one summer, or I almost did. Part of me did. I don't say that to be dramatic, only because it's true. It took me a couple years of sifting through memories and reading the journals I wrote while I was laid up in bed after it happened to understand what I lost that summer—what we all lost. Also what we gained.

My best friend, Katie Bell, and I refer to it carefully, reverently, as "that last summer." Not that it was literally my last summer, not like I'll never again have ice cream on hot August days and Fourth of July parties or swim in a clear green lake. Just that it will never be the same as it was, as it is, at Southpoint. Sometimes it makes me sad. Other times I realize there was nothing I could do. There will always be a last summer.

Reveille

The cabin is dark. The only light filters in through chinks between the gray, graffitied boards—on one side from the floodlight by the bathhouse and on the other from the moon. A few specks on my quilted bedspread of tar-colored soot from the lantern hardly bother me anymore. The mustiness of the lumpy mattress rising through the bleached sheets, the springs that jab at my hips and shoulders and squeak as I turn over in my half-sleep—these things are comforts to be called forward on cold winter nights that will come too soon.

The lake frogs like to sing to me. Chugawum wump. Chugawum wump. *They've already lullabied my friends to sleep. The girl beneath me is snoring in satisfied slumber. But anticipation of the following day slices through my log-tiredness. There will be games played with no care for a winner; laughter so deep it sharpens your breath; the sweet smell of cut grass that prickles your legs as you roll down a hill; tiny weeds whose stems wrap around their crowns and shoot flowers like fairy cannons; wild daisies in fragile chains; and sun on our backs as we search for four-leaf clovers we've never found.*

Chapter 1

*M*y foot weighed like an anchor on the accelerator as the entrance came, finally, into sight around the bend. "Camp Southpoint" read the rough hand-lettered wood sign.

As I veered onto the dusty country road that would take me home, like that old John Denver song, a growing urgency twisted my stomach. For nine years I'd bumped over this gravel road and under this tunnel of trees to my favorite place on earth. This year, though, would be different. This year I was coming to camp not as a camper. I was coming as a counselor.

I grabbed my cell phone from the empty passenger seat next to me. Only one bar. Worth a try, I thought. Keeping my eyes on the road, I deftly scrolled through my contacts. When I reached "Katie Bell," I punched

SEND, but a harsh beep informed me there was no service. I typed a quick text instead: IM HERE!!! I pressed SEND again, hoping the message would somehow find its way through satellite space, and threw my phone back onto the seat.

With nothing to occupy them, my fingers drummed the steering wheel. The music spilled from my car onto the otherwise quiet lane. IPod, not radio. If you're from Nashville—"Music City"—Tennessee, like I am, an appreciation for music is pretty much required by state law. Unfortunately, the only stations on the dial in this neck of the woods played country, and I couldn't stomach the heartsick twang of it since my father left to pursue his "singing career" and Holly, a waitress at the Bluebird Café.

I was thirteen the summer he took off. I'd bawled my head off—puffy red eyes, snot running down my face, the works—through at least four activity periods (even riding and swimming, my favorites) and three Evening Gatherings. One night after the counselor show, Katie Bell joined me on my bunk while everyone else was brushing their teeth before bed. She handed me a ball of wadded-up toilet paper and drawled in her hard-crackle country accent, "All right, Hel, that's enough."

That's when I knew Katie Bell wasn't just my

best camp friend; she was my best friend. My friends from home had tiptoed around my parents' divorce on eggshells. One "friend" had stopped talking to me altogether, probably because her mother thought I was too scandalous to associate with. But Katie Bell had barely blinked an eye. "I'm sorry, Hel," she'd said when I first told her. She'd listened to me blubber about it for three weeks, asking questions at the right parts and keeping quiet when I just needed to talk. Then she'd decided enough was enough. She followed it up by saying something so funny I actually peed in my pants. Healthy or not, that was the last time I'd cried about my dad.

I remembered that night now as I bumped down the drive. The ancient trees that lined the road into camp were a pulsating electric green. In stark contrast, I passed the rotting black stump of the tree that had been struck by lightning between camp sessions one year, and was now split down the middle. Shortly after the stump, I took a right where the lane forked and followed the gentle rain-furrowed slope of the road exactly 1.3 miles to the metal gate. Its big rusted arms were thrown open in a welcoming hug. As I slowed to bounce over the cattle guard, a smile dawned across my face. Over the low, horse-spotted hill, I could see the gleaming tin roofs of the Mansion and the Mess.

I was asked once by a friend from home "why do

you like camp so much anyway." I remembered because it had annoyed me how she had her hand on her hip as she said it. But as much as I wanted to answer, I couldn't explain the happiness and sense of relief I felt when I entered this place. During the nostalgic phone conversations that got us through the school year, Katie Bell and I often tried to put our camp experience into words. We were never quite satisfied with what came out. Our words never did it justice.

Southpoint was so much more than just a summer camp. It was a part of us that was packed up and put away when the days shortened, and the camp sheets were folded and stored in the back of the closet, and "real life" returned. Real life, with its tests and curfews and cliques and everyday dramas like runaway dads, and mothers with an ever-expanding library of self-help books. Nothing was simple in the real world. Nothing was simple like it was at Southpoint.

Which was why every June, a full two weeks before camp started, I carefully laid out and labeled my T-shirts and shorts, folded my underwear and bathing suits, packed my tennis racket and leaky swim goggles, and, come the first weekend in July, all but skipped off for five uninterrupted weeks of fun with my hundred Southpoint sisters at the southernmost point of a clear, secluded, Tennessee lake.

At camp no one knew what your dad did or if your boyfriend had just dumped you or that you'd won the sixth grade spelling bee. If they *did* know, it didn't matter. Everyone was okay here. You could be crazy or quiet—crazy got you noticed, but quiet was fine too. And shivering at ghost stories or belting out the words to campfire songs was still considered cool. The miracle of it, though, the really cool thing, I thought as I pulled up the long driveway for the first time as a counselor, was that I looked forward to camp as much at seventeen years old as I had at nine.

I pulled my car beside an old truck and climbed out, squinting in the morning sun and pushing my sunglasses from my head to the bridge of my nose. As I crossed the Yard, the large grassy area in front of the Mansion, acorns crunched under my feet. Ribbons of conversation floated out from the house's open screen doors. My pace, at the sound of familiar voices, involuntarily quickened to a trot.

The Mansion was where Southpoint's directors, Fred and Marjorie Knowles, lived during the summer. "Mansion" was a term of endearment, as the house was a pretty normal-size, squat old lodge with a large, wraparound porch. The first floor acted as infirmary, office, post office, social hub, and general Southpoint center. Before meals and Evening Gathering, girls convened in the white Adirondack chairs that populated the Yard like mushroom fairy rings.

The sudden bang of a screen door at the mess hall next door grabbed my attention. A girl appeared. I squinted (in stubborn denial of my need for contacts during the summer) and waved, even though I couldn't tell who it was. It didn't matter; everyone was family here. And I knew it couldn't be the one person I was most excited to see. Katie Bell wouldn't arrive until tomorrow, with the other campers.

With her seventeenth birthday not until September, Katie Bell had just missed the cutoff for being a junior counselor. She'd begged Fred to let her, just like he'd always let her stay in the cabin with us, even though technically she should have been in the cabin below, with the girls a year younger. He had heard her pleas sympathetically, but in the end, for insurance reasons, he explained, had to say no. That Katie Bell would be a camper for one more year, while I was a counselor, had been the agonizing topic of nearly every phone, chat, and e-mail conversation we'd had for the past year. It was my job to assure her nothing would change, but as I arrived for the first day at camp ever that I wouldn't share with Katie Bell, I wondered if I believed it myself.

The metal handle of the Mansion's screen door was

cool in my palm as I pulled it open and stepped into the dusty shade of the old house. I pushed my sunglasses back to their perch above my recently bobbed ponytail. My hair stylist (really my mom's hair stylist, whom she had recently forced on me, informing me Super Clips was no longer suitable) had been a little overzealous with my summer cut, chopping the hair I had kept long all those years for a reason, so that it barely grazed my shoulders. I hated it. It made me look six, and if I already felt terminally ordinary in appearance—with brown eyes the same nondescript shade of poo brown as my hair—this did nothing to help me out.

"Hello?" I called out, not sure whether I was on the late or early side, and which counselors might already be there.

A plump, ruddy face below a fringe of hair that reminded me of a salt-and-pepper halo poked out from behind the office door.

"Helena Waite!" Fred hurried from the office to encircle me in a bear hug.

I melted into his suntan-lotion-and-Old-Spice smell. It didn't take a degree in advanced psychology to know that Fred was a father figure to me, as he was to a lot of girls at camp.

"Hi, Fred." My greeting was muffled in his soft T-shirt.

"We're so glad you're here," he said, stepping back

to take in my one-year-older self. Sometimes I wondered if Fred and Marjorie missed us over the school year. I liked to think they did.

"That makes two of us," I answered, almost dizzy with the reality that another Southpoint summer was finally here.

"There are some girls who'll be excited to see you. Winn and Lizbeth are working on cabin assignments, if you want to see where they've put you." He nodded toward the back porch.

Then Fred glanced at his gold watch, the one he'd worn as long as I could remember. "We have a staff meeting in thirty minutes," he said. "A lot to get done before the campers get here tomorrow—but you probably have time to settle in."

The word "staff," applied to me, rang in my ears like the bugle calls that guided us through the camp day: Reveille . . . Flag Raising . . . First Call . . . Soupy . . . Tattoo . . . Taps. I realized with a buzz of excitement that those bugles wouldn't order me from place to place anymore. I was a counselor, and this Southpoint summer wouldn't be like any other.

Chapter 2

On the back porch, the one facing the lake, Winn Matthews sat curled in the seat of an Adirondack chair. Her feet were tucked up under her as she chewed on the end of a ballpoint pen. Lizbeth Waller (not *E*lizabeth, but *Liz*beth—a name I'd always thought was slightly glamorous for its omission of the first letter) sat on the top step of the porch with her back to me. They were both staring out at the lake, and when they heard my footsteps, turned.

"Lumberjack!" Winn jumped up from her seat and rushed to hug me.

"Hey!" I hugged her, then Lizbeth.

Lumberjack was a nickname she'd given me the summer before, when I was a cubby (short for "cub counselor," or what we called the oldest campers)

9

and Winn was my counselor in Cabin Nine. She said my snoring sounded like a chain saw, and did a pretty hilarious impression of these huge, snurfling wheezes that sounded like they should come from a middle-aged truck driver with sleep apnea. I guess I shouldn't have been all that surprised by the nickname. On an overnight one year, I'd snored so loudly the counselors made me move a few paces outside the circle so the other girls could sleep. Of course Katie Bell had joined me, and we'd stayed up half the night joking about our "exile."

Winn was only a year older than me, but for some reason she'd always seemed a lot older. She was the living, breathing, brochure-perfect epitome of a South-point girl. She was pretty—or pretty enough to win "prettiest" in the counselor superlatives last year—but not so freakishly pretty that you immediately had to hate her. And she did *e-very-thing* well. Riding, sailing, sports, riflery—name an activity and she had a plaque some-where at camp with her name on it.

But far more important, she did these things with a laid-back ease that suggested her successes were a result of her very nature rather than any serious effort. She knew the words to every camp song ever sung, which from some girls might be annoying, but from her was awe-inspiring. And she was funny, a quality especially prized at camp. Girls secretly pleaded to be assigned to

Winn's table at the Mess. She was like the cool older cousin you were glad was still forced to sit with you at the kids' table during holidays.

We'd bonded last summer. I wasn't sure when exactly we'd become friends, but that one day I'd crossed the line to being on her side of the joke. She'd sit on my bed before Taps, before she headed down to hang out with the other counselors at the Mansion, or borrow my iPod at rest hour. She could be unexpected and crazy at times, busting out into a funny dance or playing loud music while we cleaned for inspection. There was just something magnetic about Winn, something that drew people to her. I had a total friend-crush on her.

"You just get here?" Winn asked now.

"Yeah. Fred said you're doing cabin assignments."

Winn glanced back at two printed lists in her chair, one of campers' names and one of counselors. She sighed and said, "Unfortunately," rolling her eyes.

Southpoint's nine cabins were organized by age. Cabin One housed the youngest girls, the nine- and a few eight-year-olds, and Cabin Nine the sixteen-year-olds. Each cabin was also divided into two sides, East and West. I guess it was confusing to outsiders to hear us rattle on about Six East and Eight West—my mom *still* consistently misaddressed letters to "Helena Waite, Cabin Five North" or "Helena Waite, Cabin

Thirteen"—but for us, it was a second language.

Lizbeth scanned the counselor list for my name.

"We put you in One West," Winn said, without having to check the list. "Hope you're okay with that."

"That's great," I answered. Truthfully, Winn and Lizbeth could have put me in the barn with the horses, and I would have been enthusiastic. Just to be back at camp—and as a counselor finally—was enough.

"Awesome." Winn smiled. "Just watch out for Ellie. She's a sprinkler."

"Sprinkler?"

"Let's just say you might want to put her in a bottom bunk," Lizbeth explained, laughing. "She had some bladder control issues last summer."

"Duly noted."

Winn perched casually on the chair's armrest. Her tan legs extended like long stalks from her green shorts. "By the way, I heard Katie Bell can't be a JC with y'all."

I nodded, confirming the eminently crappy fact that Katie Bell and I wouldn't be junior counselors together.

"That sucks," said Lizbeth.

"She's not happy," I said. It was an understatement.

"Yeah, but she'll be fine," Winn assured me quickly.

For a reason I never totally understood, there was an unspoken tension between Katie Bell and Winn that had taken root last summer when Winn was our counselor and we were cubbies (me for the first and last time, and Katie Bell, apparently, for the first of two). I asked Katie Bell once why she didn't like Winn. She could only say that she didn't trust her. "Winn just wants to be liked," she'd scoffed. I personally didn't understand why that was such a bad goal (who didn't want to be liked?). But for someone like Katie Bell, who prided herself on telling it like it was even if it meant pissing you off, this wasn't just offensive, it was wrong. And Katie Bell was stubborn. If she made up her mind that something yellow was blue, you'd have better luck painting it blue than convincing her it was yellow. So I kept out of it.

Suddenly my butt vibrated. I jumped, forgetting that I'd slid my phone into my back pocket, and quickly flipped it open. One new message from Katie Bell: SO JEALOUS. C U 2MORO!!!

I smiled. "Speak of the devil."

"Careful not to let Fred see that," warned Winn, pointing at my phone. She'd picked up her two lists again. "He's on a rant this year about all the kids wanting to bring their cell phones to camp. Some parent called to see if her daughter could have special permission."

"Really?" I glanced around and quickly deposited the phone back in my pocket. I'd turn it off and keep it in my car. It was the last thing I'd need these five weeks.

"I think Pookie and Lila need help sweeping out the Craft Shop," Winn said, talking about two other JCs. She frowned down at her list.

"Which campers should we put in Three East this year?" she asked Lizbeth. "Janie requested to be with Lizzie, but Lizzie wants to be with Kate, and Kate and Janie don't get along. . . . Maybe once you've dropped your stuff at your cabin you can help them at the Craft Shop?"

I realized Winn was talking to me again. "Oh! Sure."

"'Kay." She smiled. "See ya at the meeting."

I skipped off the porch steps as if the sound track to *The Sound of Music* was on a loop in my head, down the path that circled the Mansion—*The hills are alive!*—and back to my car to take my trunk to Cabin One West. It was good to be home.

It seemed the other counselors weren't quite as enthused as I was about all the work that had to be done before the campers arrived the next morning. It probably indicates some deep-seated psychological issue, but I get pleasure out of chores. I'd been making Katie Bell's bed for inspection for years, hospital corners being a secret fetish of mine. My mom was thrilled when I first came home from camp wrapping the corners of my bed like origami. Then she started worrying I might be

OCD. I realized this when I found *Dr. Wong's Guide to Understanding Your Child with Obsessive Compulsive Disorder* on her bedside table.

I'd never thought to consider what went into opening a camp after three intervening seasons had had their way. There were cabins to be unlocked and mouse poop to be swept, flypaper to be hung from the rafters with care, and bathrooms to be cleaned. There were musty mattresses to be aired and bunk beds to be accounted for, floating docks to be moored, stalls to be mucked, sailboats to be taken out of dry dock—not to mention two counselor meetings, the one that had just ended being a three-hour marathon.

Some of the exhausted counselors had stuck around the Mess after the meeting ended, but by eleven thirty the only brave souls who remained to raid the Mess pantry were Winn, Lizbeth, their friend Sarah, and myself.

The conversation had turned from an all-out bitch session about chores, and a unanimous decision that fly paper was invented by a sadistic and severely disturbed man, into a brainstorm for pranks to pull on our brother camp across the lake.

Southpoint and Camp Brownstone shared a boating program and weekly dances, during which we alternately ignored and fell in love with Brownstone boys and, more often, their counselors. My personal Brownstone obsession was Ransome Knowles, the son of Brownstone's director and Fred's brother, Abe. Ransome (even his *name* was hot) had been the object of my affection from a time before I even knew what you *did* with boys (not that I was exactly an expert now).

"Brownies," as we called the Brownstone counselors, and "Pointers," as they called us, also shared a longstanding prank war.

Cross-legged on top of one of the Mess's long wooden tables, Winn dipped a large serving spoon into an economy-size jar of peanut butter. "What about a good old-fashioned panty raid?" she asked, drawing the spoon from the peanut butter and licking it like a lollipop.

"Eww." Lizbeth crinkled her nose in disgust.

"The idea of Brownie panties or my peanut butter?" asked Winn.

"Both," said Sarah. "And do you have to use the word *panty*?"

"Panty, panty, panty," Winn chanted, laughing. As she did, Lizbeth mashed the spoonful of peanut butter against Winn's mouth, smearing the sticky brown stuff over the bottom half of her face and chin.

Winn jerked away, still laughing, with her eyes closed and her mouth hanging open, a melting glob of unswallowed peanut butter inside. She reached into the jar and made a retaliatory swipe across Lizbeth's face. Lizbeth shrieked in disbelief before cracking up.

Noticing my amusement and relative unstickiness, Winn wiped some peanut butter from her own face and lunged at my my hair. Just barely, I dodged her, and Winn's outstretched hand landed instead on Sarah's bare forearm.

"Hey!" Sarah protested, but just as she was about to return the favor, Winn hissed a sharp "Shhh!" and cocked her ear to listen.

We froze, trying to stifle our giggles and listen at the same time.

"Did you hear Fred?" I whispered. The last thing I wanted was to get in trouble my very first night as a counselor.

For a moment, there was a strained silence. Then Winn broke it.

"Ha-ha!" She laughed. "Gotchy'all."

"You bitch!" Lizbeth cried. She screwed the top onto the peanut butter and went to put it in the pantry. I heard the spoon clatter in the bottom of the kitchen sink.

"But seriously," said Winn, cleaning her face with a paper towel she had grabbed from the top of the milk dispenser we called "the silver cow," "we have to focus. I *know* Buzz and Nate are already planning their first prank on us. Disaster preparedness is the first line of defense."

Buzz and Nate were two Brownies who worked on the waterfront with Ransome. (I was sadly *way* too aware of any and all things Ransome-related.)

"I know," said Sarah, "but we have the same problem as last year. How do we get over there without the campers seeing us?"

"How'd you pull it off last time?" I asked. The previous summer, Southpoint had buzzed with the news that the counselors had replaced Brownstone's Stars and Stripes with a bright pink flag featuring a unicorn and a happy rainbow.

"We dressed as guys from the cleaners that pick up their laundry," said Winn. "They leave their laundry bags at the base of the flagpole. They didn't realize what had hit them till a JC took the flag down that night."

"Aha." I nodded thoughtfully. "Undercover."

Lizbeth suddenly started laughing as she remembered something funny. "One of the campers even walked up with a laundry bag he'd forgotten to put out and handed it to Winn."

Winn gagged. "It smelled like dirty feet and olives."

The wheels in my head had already started turning. *The Parent Trap* was my favorite movie as a kid—the old version, not the one with Lindsay Lohan before she got boobs and discovered leggings. I used to imagine I was Hayley Mills and, for lack of siblings to torture, would try to play pranks on my parents. Sadly, they always failed, and my dad grounded me more than once for putting Saran Wrap over his toilet seat. But the point was, I'd been in training for this mission since I could say the words "duct tape."

"What if we sneak over while they're here for a dance?" I asked.

Winn raised a mischievous eyebrow. "I like where you're going with this. . . ."

"And do something to their beds," I finished.

"Like short-sheet them?" asked Sarah dubiously.

"Or put itching powder in them?" said Winn.

"Or move them completely." I smiled impishly. "To the floating dock."

"Yesss!" Winn lit up, slapping her leg so hard it had to have left a mark. "That's perfect!"

Sarah frowned. "How would we get the beds to the floating dock?"

I explained. "We could only put one or two on the floating dock—"

"Buzz's," all three of them said at once.

"And we'd just balance the mattress between two canoes and row it out there."

"Awesome!" said a satisfied Lizbeth.

Sarah clapped, and Winn had a new gleam in her eyes.

The plan of attack decided upon, we faded quickly. We stood, stretching and yawning, and moved to put the evidence of our pig-out session—graham crackers, potato chips, chocolate bars for s'mores, mugs of hot chocolate and milk—away.

"Do we need to clean these?" I asked, setting my chipped ceramic mug in the bottom of the kitchen's industrial-size sink with the rest of the mismatched dishes.

Winn waved her hand. "We'll get them tomorrow morning," she said authoritatively. "I have to be down here to finish name tags at the butt-crack of dawn anyway."

We all shuffled, exhausted from the day, to the Mess door. Winn, the last one out, flipped the switch, and the dining hall went dark as the screen door slammed behind us. Across camp, the only visible light came from the floodlight by the Bath. Suddenly I noticed the stars above us. They were out in magnificent numbers, a blanket of lights.

Quietly, we filed down the path from the Mansion to the Bath, where we brushed our teeth and washed our faces. As each girl finished, hanging her washcloth on a nail to dry, or clicking her toothbrush against the porcelain sink before putting it up, she whispered "Good night" and made her way up the low hill to the cabins.

As I turned to do the same, something suddenly struck me as odd. It wasn't just being at camp without campers or hanging out in the Mess way after our usual bedtime. It was that there was no Taps to send us to sleep. Obviously Fred wouldn't blow the bugle until the campers arrived. The empty cabins, and horses in the barn, didn't need a bugle to tell them what time of day it was. I smiled to myself when I realized I'd always imagined Fred blew the bugle every day, not just when we were there. I'd seen Reveille and Taps as unstoppable forces of nature. Tonight, though, we would sneak to our cabins in silence, with nothing but the sounds of crickets and lake frogs in our ears.

Chapter 3

The next morning I sat on the steps of Cabin One with Pookie, the counselor for One East, waiting for our campers to show. A ball of tired, nervous excitement radiated from the pit of my stomach. I searched the line of cars crawling up the road toward the cabins for the Bells' monster of a truck, but saw no sign of Katie Bell. As the girls in my cabin arrived, towing trunks and tennis racquets and parents, I had to give up my post, knowing anyway that Katie Bell was always late on opening day.

By mid-morning, three returning nine-year-olds had laid claim to bunks, expertly showing their parents how to slide their trunks beneath the bed. Two more girls were just arriving, both frys—Southpoint-speak for "first-year camper." One of them recognized a friend, threw open her car door, and dashed to Two East, leaving her dad to carry her overloaded trunk into the cabin. I apologized when he bumped his head on the low door.

The second girl was small, with white-blond hair that sprouted in a tangle of ringlets around her nervous face. She climbed reluctantly from the backseat of her parents' SUV, cautiously surveying the activity around her. From the name tag she'd been handed at the front gate and had dutifully pinned to her lime green shirt, I was able to identify her as Ruby Standish, turned nine years old this month, from Huntsville, Alabama.

I knelt down in front of her so that our faces were level. "Hi, Ruby. I'm Helena," I said brightly. "I'll be your counselor this summer."

Ruby pursed her lips. Fidgeting with a loop on her shorts, she stared at me, wide-eyed and suspicious.

A tanned freckled hand landed on Ruby's shoulder. "Ruby's a little shy," her mother explained. "But you're excited about your first summer at camp, aren't you, sweetie?" she said to Ruby.

Ruby looked up at her mother and nodded slowly.

"She just needs some time to adjust," Mrs. Standish whispered.

I smiled in understanding. "Would you like me to show you the cabin?" I asked Ruby.

She nodded and, when I reached for her hand, didn't resist. Glancing back at her parents only once, she followed me into the simple cabin that we'd both call home for the next five weeks.

"It smells funny." Ruby wrinkled her nose at the smell of wood, dirt, and dust that, try as we might, could never be completely swept out.

For me, the worn plank floors, buckling cubbyholes, sagging bunk beds, and screened windows were comforting. Still, remembering back to my first summer, when Sally McDougal had shown me this same cabin, I could see how foreign and spare it must have looked to Ruby.

I laughed at her pinched expression. "You'll get used to it," I promised.

I settled Ruby into the bunk next to mine and directed her parents to the Bath, where campers were supposed to take their toiletries. As I watched them walk down the hill, Ruby holding a hand on either side, I had to shield my eyes from the sun. It was directly overhead now, and still no Katie Bell. My eyes swept from the lake, just visible through a stand of trees to the right of the cabins, to a knot of girls hugging each other as they jumped up and down, to two young campers flying down the hill toward the footbridge that led to—

"Ransome." The sound of a deep male voice stopped my heart. I held my breath as I watched a tan, wiry frame carrying a trunk swing around to reveal *his* face. Ransome. My stomach fluttered.

Abe always sent a few Brownstone counselors over on opening day to help carry trunks. We pretended to resent the implication that we couldn't handle them on our own, but in the oppressive July heat, we were secretly more than happy to watch the boys sweat it out. I'd play damsel in distress any day if it meant seeing Ransome.

The hottest counselors were like Greek gods to us, and our crushes were no less fervent for the fact that they would never be fulfilled. This over-the-top ego boost was probably the only reason Brownies fought tooth and nail over the honor of lugging our eighty-pound trunks in hundred-degree weather and taking giggly screaming girls for inner-tube rides.

Technically, Ransome was only three years and two grades older than I was, but in my mind, he was light-years more mature and equally out of reach. Still, unlike some lucky girls, my improbable crush had not faded over the years. It might have even gotten worse. Watching from Cabin One's porch, my heart beat like a bongo drum in my chest as the sweat beaded below Ransome's close-cropped, copper-brown hair and dripped down his forehead and over the tip of his straight, noble nose. What was cuter than a guy willing to haul a ten-year-old's trunk full of too many T-shirts and a year's supply of socks? I wondered.

I was lost in my favorite dream sequence (all hazy light and slow motion), in which Ransome turns, finally recognizes the goddess of a woman I have become—Aphrodite to his Adonis—tosses the trunk like it weighs no more than a feather, and runs to sweep me off my flip-flops and into his arms, when—

"Hel!" My thoughts were interrupted again. "Hel!"

Before I even turned to see her hanging half out of her parents' car window, waving her arms and beaming, I knew Katie Bell's voice. I launched off the porch steps toward the fire engine–red truck, from which Katie Bell jumped before it had come to a complete stop. When I picked her up to hug her, Katie Bell's feet literally left the ground. At five eight, I'd long ago surpassed her in height. One of our favorite games was for me to fling her across my back and spin in circles until she begged me to stop under threat of vomiting and we both collapsed to the ground in hysterics.

"Where have you been?" I demanded.

Katie Bell jerked her thumb at her four younger brothers spilling out of the truck. "You know how the Bell clan moves."

Katie Bell's full name was actually Katherine Clarke Bell, but everyone, even her own family, called her

Katie Bell, as if it were a double name.

As we hugged again, the second-youngest Bell, Bobby, raced past us, chasing his brother Red. I never understood how "Red" had been saved for the youngest Bell, as every kid in the family, including Katie Bell, had a head of auburn hair and a constellation of freckles just like their mother. I liked to imagine there'd been some kind of family meeting or a drawing of straws.

"Hi, Mrs. Bell," I said politely as Katie Bell's mom approached. She was a substantial woman in Wrangler jeans and a sleeveless tank top that revealed doughy, white arms.

Mrs. Bell smiled and pulled me in for a hug, the real eye-popping kind that shows you mean it. "Hi, darlin'."

The Bells were *country*, and it tickled me. Mrs. Bell had always been sweet to me, especially after my parents' divorce, when she started addressing care packages to "Helena Waite and her friend Katie Bell." That was just the kind of people the Bells were—sugar and spice.

They lived on the family farm outside of Knoxville, where they grew soybeans. I'd seen the Bell farm twice, once when my dad brought me along on a business trip to Knoxville, and the second time the year I'd gotten my driver's license. Katie Bell had been to Nashville too.

Her parents had let her take the Greyhound when she was fourteen, which had scandalized my mother but awed me.

"Katie Bell, which cabin you say you're in?" Mr. Bell was huffing and puffing with her trunk. "Hey there, Miss Helena."

"Hi, Mr. Bell."

"Nine, Dad," Katie Bell grumbled. "Cabin Nine. Again. 'Cause I'm the oldest frikkin' camper known to man."

Katie Bell had a flair for the dramatic and a habit of throwing out unnecessary superlatives. This time, however, she *was* the oldest camper known to Southpoint, if not the world.

"Katie Bell," I pleaded, "come on. It's not that bad. It'll be kind of fun."

She raised an auburn eyebrow and searched my face skeptically. There was no bullshitting Katie Bell. Her stormy blue eyes that she called "gunmetal gray" were disconcerting when they flashed on you unexpectedly. Like they were doing now.

"I still can't believe it," she drawled, her lip curling at the inhumanity of it all. "After eight years together, they split up Hels Bells."

"Hel" was what Katie Bell had started calling me the summer I was ten and she was nine, and we thought it was a cool way to say "hell" without ending up there. "Hels Bells" was what we insisted on calling ourselves as a pair. At first it had amused us to no end. Then it was just second nature.

"Katie Bell," I started, ready to convince her once again that she'd hardly notice the camper-counselor divide, when she interrupted me.

"Hel, there he is!" She dug her fingernails into my arm and nodded over my shoulder.

I didn't have to turn. I knew who she was talking about, and my face flushed instantly.

"Shhh! I know. How hot does he look?" I asked, rhetorically of course.

Katie Bell gave Ransome a slinky once-over with her eyes, and jokingly gnashed her teeth like a hungry puma that had just spotted its prey. Being discreet was not one of her strong points.

I laughed and slapped her across the arm. "Hands off," I joked. "He's mine."

"Well, you *are* a counselor now. . . ." she said through a lopsided grin.

"Shut up," I sighed. "Ransome doesn't even know who I am. He probably thinks I'm still just another camper."

Katie Bell's jaw tightened. She jerked her shoulder into a shrug, dropping it. Winn and Sarah had strolled up.

"Heeey!" Winn chimed. She locked a stiff Katie Bell in an awkward hug.

"Hey," Katie Bell replied.

"So you're back in Nine East again!"

"Yeah," Katie Bell said with markedly less enthusiasm. "I'm thinking about taking up permanent residence."

"Well, take care of it for me," said Winn. "I switched to Cabin Five this year."

"I'll try." Katie Bell responded to her light tone with a flatness I hoped Winn didn't notice.

Winn turned to me. "When all your girls are here, we're supposed to tell them to meet on the Yard. There should be a bugle soon."

I nodded, although Winn's reminder was unnecessary. I'd been through this drill every year too, as a camper. "My girls are all down there already, I think."

"Then do you want to come with us now?" asked Sarah.

I glanced at Katie Bell.

"Go ahead," she answered. "I still have to find my Bath locker and take my riding stuff to the barn." Katie Bell rode horses at home and competed during the year. Most of her free activity periods she spent at the barn.

I snapped my fingers. "Oh, that reminds me. Cabin

Nine's supposed to put their stuff on top of the lockers this year. We ran out of space."

Katie Bell nodded, her mouth a strange squiggly line on her pale, lightly freckled face. "Thanks."

"I'll see you down at the Yard?" I asked, already turning to follow Winn and Sarah down the hill.

"Sure," Katie Bell called. "Guess I'll see y'all there."

It was hard for me to pick a favorite day at camp, but opening night was a definite contender for the title. Most of our Evening Gatherings would take place at the Bowl, an amphitheater-shaped grassy area below the Mansion, but opening night took place at the bonfire pit by the lake.

After dinner, Katie Bell and I wandered together down the pine needle–covered path to the lake. Almost all the rough log benches surrounding the fire pit were already occupied when we arrived. Campers and counselors talked excitedly, waiting for Fred and Marjorie's arrival.

Katie Bell and I found a spot between two of the benches and settled into our folding camping chairs. I leaned back, balancing in the chair and tilting my face to the sky. Above us there was nothing but purple sky ringed by pine trees. I filled my lungs with the fresh air and held my breath, imagining the air swirling through my body, around my chest, and down my legs into my toes, clearing out all the cobwebs and breathing into the dark places.

"I love the smell of camp," said Katie Bell, reading my mind.

"Me too."

"Oh!" Katie Bell cried suddenly. It startled me. "What happened with John? You didn't e-mail me back the other day."

"That." I rolled my eyes. "Yeah, sorry. I was packing and then forgot. He texted to say, 'Have fun at camp,' but I didn't text him back."

"Why not?"

"I'm just over it."

"You never seemed that under it," Katie Bell observed, fiddling with the strap on her chair.

"I guess 'cause I wasn't." I laughed. "How did that horse show go last week?"

"Fine. I didn't place, though."

"That sucks," I observed brilliantly. Katie Bell normally won her horse shows.

"Eh." She shrugged.

We settled into a comfortable silence, listening to the girls around us talk and the birds sing in the trees. It was funny to know the ins and outs of each other's lives without ever having laid eyes on most of the people or places we told each other about. Of course Katie Bell knew all about John. He and I had dated for four months that spring—in the pseudo way we dated at home, where "going out" meant hooking up with someone on a regular basis, with the occasional movie thrown in to make it official. But he'd never given me butterflies. Sometimes making out with him felt like kissing my brother —if I'd had a brother. By the end of the school year, I guess we'd both given up. When he just stopped calling, I had a panicky moment of fear that he was the love of my life, which reignited the flame for about a week. It promptly burned out again. I acted pissed when we broke up for good, because my friends made me feel like that's how I was supposed to be, but honestly, it felt almost obligatory. And with camp on the horizon, I'd already resumed my fantasizing about Ransome. Katie Bell knew that too.

Suddenly the sound of a dog barking rose above the talking, and the whole atmosphere in the clearing changed. Fred and Marjorie were coming, trailed by their yellow Lab, Butter. Fred was carrying the bugle and a torch he'd use to light the bonfire. We fell silent in anticipation, the only sound coming from the wind in the trees, until Butter ran and jumped onto a counselor named Caroline, and everyone laughed.

Fred handed the torch to Marjorie and walked to the

top of the fire pit, so that the lake was at his back. We watched expectantly as he raised the dented brass bugle to his lips. He puffed out his cheeks and launched into a familiar tune. We cheered as his face turned red and his chest expanded for each rolling refrain.

At the end, a breathless Fred lowered the bugle. "Camp Southpoint's fifty-seventh summer is now officially in session!" he called proudly to the tops of the pines.

"Wooo!" Girls whooped and yelled and clapped. Katie Bell put her fingers in her mouth and let out an ear-piercing whistle.

Fred traded Marjorie the bugle for the torch and raised the orange flame high above his head. "As most of you know," he said, smiling out at ninety-three campers and twenty-one counselors—his one hundred fourteen daughters for the summer, "we like to start our Southpoint summers with a ceremonial bonfire. Marjorie and I"—Fred glanced back at his wife, who smiled as she rubbed Butter's grizzled old head—"expect this camp session to be the best yet. We hope and pray that it will be happy and healthy and full of fun. And we like to take this night to remember—and to show our first-year campers—what it is that makes this place so special: friendship."

Though Fred never asked—it wasn't a religious camp—

we bowed our heads as if we were at church. I suppose, in that moment, in a way we were. For me, this ground was more hallowed than any pew I'd ever been forced into.

Fred continued. "Mother Nature, thank you for holding us in your embrace as we come together for another camp session. We ask that you keep us safe, shelter us from the storms, and lift us up in the spirit of friendship and family."

"Amen," a few girls murmured reflexively under their breath.

Silently, Fred took the torch and very slowly circled the firewood stacked like a teepee in the center of the clearing, touching the flame to the dry wood. As it crackled and hissed, gray smoke curled up into the clear sky. Katie Bell and I both held out our arms to compare goose bumps.

When the bonfire had caught and was starting to burn strong, Fred threw the torch into the flames and went to stand again next to Marjorie. In her hand she held a metal pail with the words "Camp Southpoint" stenciled on it, filled with seeds and dried corn kernels. We knew the routine. Wordlessly, the entire camp lined up in front of Marjorie, so that every camper and counselor could reach into the bucket for a handful. One by one, we would file past the fire and reverently toss our seeds into the flames. We were "sowing our dreams for the summer," Marjorie said. I always thrilled at the snap-crackle-pop that they made.

After sacrificing my seeds to the fire, I took my place next to Katie Bell in the circle that was forming around the bonfire. By now it was burning brightly against the lowering dusk.

When the last girl had gone, Fred and Marjorie threw their seeds into the fire and took the hands of the campers next to them so that the entire camp stood hand in hand in an unbroken circle.

The older counselors nodded and, as one, we began to sing. First we would sing Southpoint's official song, the one written by Fred's father when *his* father started Southpoint. Southpoint girls had sung these lyrics at every opening and closing ceremony for fifty-seven years.

"Hail to Camp Southpoint, near our hearts to thee!" Our voices grew stronger and louder as we sang and the words flooded back from the corners of our minds, where they'd been stored all year. "The place where our hearts abide, a haven from the rising tide. Oh Southpoint, oh Southpoint, your friendship comforts me. . . ."

First-year campers watched and listened, absorbing the words as the older girls sang by heart, making faces around the circle at their friends, and squeezing each others' hands.

When the final solemn verse was sung, it was time for the tearjerker—the other song we sang at both opening and closing ceremonies, "Friends." Only, at the end of camp, the song's words would be much more poignant, because we'd know it would be another year before we sang them again.

Our volume swelled as the chorus started. Lips were trembling. My vision blurred as the tears welled, and when Katie Bell squeezed my hand, I was a goner. One lone tear tumbled down my cheek, followed in quick succession by a river of its fat siblings.

If it had been only me blubbering like an idiot, I would have felt stupid, but directly across the circle I saw Winn, Sarah, and Lizbeth, all hand in hand and all crying. Knowing that others felt the same happiness and relief and sadness—that in just five short weeks it would all be over for another forty-seven—made me feel okay.

At the end of the song, the circle broke as girls turned to one another, hugging and laughing and wiping the tears from their cheeks, reminding each other that this was the *happy* time we sang this song. We had a whole Southpoint summer ahead of us.

It was growing dark now. The night was almost velvety around us. We took our seats again around the light of the campfire. A few counselors, including Winn, bunched close to the fire so we could see them as they led us in other, more boisterous, camp songs. We sang "Boom Chicka Boom," "Do Your Ears Hang Low?" "Titanic," "The Song That Never Ends" (it did, finally), "Have You Ever Gone Fishin'?" "A Boy and a Girl in a Little Canoe" (I loved that one), and "The Cutest Boy I Ever Saw." All songs I knew by heart.

Across the still darkness of the water, through the trees, I could just make out a twin to our fire, burning alluringly on the opposite side of the lake. It was Brownstone's opening ceremony, and I found myself thinking of Ransome. I wondered if he had, like me, made a wish as he threw his handful of seeds into the fire. My wish, of course, cast him in a starring role, although I couldn't imagine I'd play even a bit part in his. I wondered if the boys were also singing songs. I wondered if Ransome was leading, or if he sat, content like me next to his best friend, letting the familiar words and the night wrap around him like a soft old blanket.

After Evening Gathering, Katie Bell and I sat on my cabin porch talking and watching the campers wander up from the Bath. We were already a good way into the candy stash that Katie Bell had brought from home and that was supposed to last us five weeks.

Katie Bell was convulsing, she was laughing so hard. "And then," she gasped, remembering the time I'd been cast by my cabin as Austin Powers for an Evening Gathering game of "Guess Who," although I'd never even seen the movies, "you did this awkward pelvic thrust when you said, 'Yeah, baby.'" She stood up for a wildly spastic impersonation of me doing a spastic impersonation.

"Stop!" I pleaded. My stomach hurt from the deep silent laughter shaking my body. That Evening Gathering had been one of the more mortifying moments of my life.

We were wiping our eyes and catching our breath, when Tattoo blew. Almost time for lights out. Heaving a dramatic sigh, Katie Bell tromped off to Cabin Nine with a "G'night, Hel."

She had just left when Winn, passing by on the way to her cabin, stopped in front of my porch.

"Hey," she said.

Behind me I could hear the scrape of my campers' trunks and the squeak of their bedsprings as they got ready for bed. I had lit the old-fashioned kerosene lantern that hung from the center rafter so they could see, and Winn was bathed in the yellowish glow that escaped through the cabin's open doorway and screened windows.

"Hey," I said. "What's up?"

"I wanted to let you know that a few counselors are going down to the riflery range tonight," Winn whispered in a low, confidential voice.

"The riflery range?"

"Sometimes we meet Brownies there to hang out after Taps."

We'd always wondered what the counselors did when they left us sleeping under the watchful eyes of the CODs (Southpoint code for Counselors on Duty—the two counselors who had to stay around the cabins after Taps in case something happened or a camper got sick.) But it was like thinking about what your parents did before you were born. You wanted to know, but maybe you kind of didn't either.

Now that I thought about it, the riflery range was the perfect rendezvous point. It was at the edge of both camps, where their boundaries met, and far enough away from the cabins and the Mansion that you wouldn't have to be afraid of Fred or Abe or the campers hearing you.

"If you wanna come," Winn offered, "I'll swing by your cabin later. . . ."

My heart spazzed in my chest. *Of course* I wanted to go. Ransome might be there.

"I gotta get to my cabin," Winn said, hesitating for my answer.

"Yes! Yeah, I want to go," I stammered. "Will you come get me?"

"Sure. I'll be by after Taps."

I nodded, and Winn slid away into the darkness.

Chapter 4

*A*s my hiking boots slushed through the field toward the riflery range, my stomach churned. Other than camp dances, which totally didn't count, this would be my first time hanging out with Brownies.

I had guy friends at home, of course. And there were boyfriends. John, and Tyler before him, and a boy named Alex who lived in my neighborhood. But they weren't Brownies. Brownies were a different species of male entirely. They were a lost tribe of boys who were much cooler, much hotter, and much more elusive than the ones who roamed the real world. They were more desirable for the fact that they were always present but out of reach. At least they had been—until now.

Slightly ahead of me, Winn and Sarah bushwhacked their way through the overgrown grass. We'd left a jealous Lizbeth behind as a COD.

In the near distance, under the squat silhouette of the riflery hut, red pinpoints of light danced in chaotic circles like drunk lightning bugs. It took me a second to realize—as the muffled conversation became clearer and unraveled into individual voices, male and female— that the dancing red lightning bugs were cigarette butts. If Fred caught us sneaking out *and* smoking, he'd surely have no choice but to kick us out. The risk was both nauseatingly scary and electrifying.

"Hey," a low male voice said as we approached. In the watery moonlight I could make out the owner of the voice as Buzz. It wasn't his real name, obviously, just a nickname, and the only one he used at camp. He was one of the waterfront counselors who came to South-point to take the girls out on the motorboats. He was short and muscley with cropped brown hair, close-set eyes, and a square jaw that reminded me of a bulldog.

He was sitting on the dusty riflery hut floor next to Ransome. My eyes rested on Ransome and then quickly darted away.

"What took y'all so long?" Ransome asked us.

The self-assurance behind his question—the impli-cation that Ransome knew what it took to sneak out of camp late at night, having done it so many times him-self he could calculate how long it should take and how easy it should be—kind of thrilled me.

Winn and Sarah settled into spaces left between the guys and the handful of older girl counselors who'd gotten there before us. I suddenly felt like the last one standing in Musical Chairs, turning around and around in my little spot as I hunted for a place to sit. Seeing me spinning like a top, Ransome slid over on one of the rotting, water-stained mattresses we used for campers who had to lie down to shoot the heavy guns.

"Here ya go, Helena," he said as he readjusted, leaving a tight wedge where I could just barely fit my butt.

I froze, my cheeks burning at the discovery that Ransome knew my name. Was I still wearing my name tag from opening day? I panicked and looked down. I wasn't.

"Thanks," I stammered, and smiled sheepishly as I squeezed myself onto the mattress. I pulled my knees in tight to keep from crowding him.

"Welcome to the range. It's kinda tight, but we manage."

I'd seen Ransome a thousand times before, but I realized I could count on two hands the number of times I had heard him speak. His voice was deeper than I'd remembered. He smelled like sweat, but the good kind of sweat—the kind you work up from being outside in the sun all day carrying little girls' trunks for them. There was another smell mingling in there too, and I realized it was dip. A wad of the pungent black stuff, which had always reminded me of mulch, protruded from his bottom lip. As I watched him out of the corner of my eye, he raised an empty Gatorade bottle to his mouth and spit, the brown juice oozing down the side of the bottle. It was gross, but I ignored it. There was not much Ransome Knowles could do that would turn me off. Possibly farting the "Star Spangled Banner" while kicking puppies. Possibly.

I think it was Winn who had the idea to play "Never Have I Ever." I hadn't played before, so Sarah filled me in. We'd go around the circle, each person saying something he or she had never done, and those who *had* done it had to raise their hands. Normally, Winn explained, it was a drinking game, the purpose of which was to get the "worst" players drunk.

Half an hour later, an older counselor named Marge cocked her head as she tried to think of one no one had said yet. "Never, never have I ever . . . made out in the Craft Shop."

Since we didn't have alcohol, the purpose of our game was apparently just to call each other out on embarrassing stuff we'd done. Not all of us at the riflery range, however, were so easily embarrassed. A Brownie named Will threw up his hand, followed by

Buzz and, grudgingly, Sarah. Winn and a few of the other counselors busted out laughing. I wished I could see their faces better. They knew something I didn't.

"All right. I've got one," said Winn. She arched an eyebrow and smirked at Ransome. "Never, never have I ever been busted by Abe while hooking up on a camp boat."

Buzz elbowed Ransome in the ribs, and he reluctantly raised his hand.

"It wasn't during camp!" Ransome protested.

"Are you sure about that?" Buzz goaded.

"I promise." Ransome was laughing now. I could feel his body shaking next to mine.

It was ridiculous to feel jealous, but I didn't like knowing that Ransome had hooked up with someone— anyone. Even stranger was knowing that everyone else, like Winn, knew about it.

As the game went on, I started to feel like a prude. The exploits admitted by everyone around me were like badges of honor, not scarlet letters. It made me wish I was one of those girls who bent the rules more often, who snuck out at night and answered dares with an attitude that said, "Watch me." So I got a little carried away in the laughter and once—maybe twice—raised my hand for things I'd never come close to doing. In the moment it didn't seem to matter that I was lying. Out here at the riflery range that smelled like gunpowder and was littered with spent bullet shells, we were a band of thieves creating our own legends.

But it was something I *didn't* raise my hand for, chickening out at the last minute, too scared I might get caught, that got Ransome's attention.

"Lumberjack, you've never been skinny-dipping in the lake?" Winn asked when I was the only one who didn't raise my hand to Sarah's "Never, never."

I shook my head, my face flushing at Winn's use of the less than flattering nickname in front of Ransome. Never, never had I ever been in the lake after dark. After sundown the waterfront was strictly off-limits to campers.

Now everyone was looking at me. "No." I heard my voice falter. "Never been skinny-dipping." I tried to recover with confidence.

"Well, Lumberjack," Ransome said, raising an eyebrow and spitting again into his dip bottle, "we'll have to change that before the summer's over."

I thought—but couldn't be sure without seeing his face—that Ransome . . . was flirting. Oh my God, my mind raced. Why? How? What?! I couldn't be making it up. There was an unmistakable attraction or electricity or *something* that flowed across the short space between us. *Say something*, I commanded myself. Don't let this chance slip away.

"Better hurry," I joked. "We only have four weeks and six days left." Oh, it was lame—so lame—and a few seconds too late, like I'd been formulating my response too long, but thankfully Ransome laughed anyway.

He turned to grin at me—a huge, beaming smile. For some reason, in the moonlight, what I noticed were his teeth. They were perfectly white and straight, except for one on the side, which stuck out at an angle, disrupting the whole symmetry of his mouth in an adorable, approachable way.

"Well, all right then," Ransome challenged. "I didn't realize we were on a timetable. Next time we're going skinny-dipping," he announced, turning to confirm this with the other counselors still there.

My heart thudded so loudly in my ears I was afraid everyone could hear it. "All right then," I said.

"Got one!" Winn interjected suddenly. "Never, never have I ever . . ."

The night slid by until the game wound down and the cigarettes ran out. People drifted back to their respective camps and cabins, complaining that Reveille would blow in just a matter of hours. Already I knew I wouldn't be able to sleep even for the few precious ones we had left.

Using a flashlight I'd borrowed from Ruby, I helped Winn pluck the cigarette butts from the cracks in the riflery hut's plank floor. Even a single butt left behind would be a giveaway to the first activity group in the morning, so we had to be thorough. Looking for something to put the stinky butts in, I searched the floor and ledges around me.

"Here," Ransome said, offering his dip bottle. When I reflexively squinched my nose at the disgusting inch of brown viscous liquid in the bottom, he laughed and instead held out his hand. As I tipped my palm to let the butts fall into his, our fingers touched. It was only a second, but again I felt the current pass through me.

"Thanks." I smiled and quickly looked away, embarrassed at how obvious I felt my attraction had to be.

Ransome put the butts one by one into the dip bottle and, after tightly screwing on the top, slid the bottle into the pocket of his baggy, stained khakis. Buzz was waiting for him on the path back to Brownstone.

"Good night, y'all," Ransome said, ducking to clear the roof of the hut and loping toward Buzz.

"Sleep tight." It slipped. It was the last thing my father used to say to me before bed. While my dad had left me, the habit hadn't. I cringed now at how childish it sounded.

But again Ransome surprised me. "Don't let the bedbugs bite," he called before being swallowed up by the pines and dark. My heart nearly exploded.

"You ready?" Winn asked. Sarah had already left, bored with the final rounds of the game.

"Yep," I answered, still unable to wipe the smile from my face. Without thinking, I swung the beam of the flashlight around to light our way back to the cabins.

"No," Winn startled me by saying sharply. She jumped to switch the flashlight's power button off. "Campers might see it," she explained, sounding apologetic for her brusque tone.

"Oh, right." My head was swimming with the crazy notion that Ransome wasn't someone I had to just admire from afar anymore. "I wasn't thinking. Sorry."

"Don't worry." Winn sighed, entwining her arm in mine and turning us toward the shadowy path back to the cabins. "You'll learn, little grasshopper."

The only thing I was worried about was seeing Ransome again, but I hoped she was right. As a counselor, there was still a lot I didn't know.

Chapter 5

$\mathcal{I}$ had been wrong when I thought, returning from the riflery range, that I wouldn't be able to fall asleep. When I slipped quietly into my bed, not even bothering to change my clothes, just removing my smoky fleece and kicking off my boots, all the excitement of the last two days caught up with me. As soon as my head hit the pillow, I fell into an exhausted, dreamless sleep.

I woke to the sound of Reveille the next morning, and the day began like any other at camp. Bleary-eyed and rumpled, I slipped on my flip-flops and padded with the other girls to the flagpole that stood always at attention in a clearing at the middle of the cabins. In front of it were a very chipper Marjorie and Butter.

Once we had all lined up, Marjorie placed her hand over her heart. We followed her lead as two counselors carefully unfolded and raised a large American flag. When the metal of the clasps clinked against the top of the pole, and Old Glory hung limply in the windless morning, we launched into a plodding recitation of the Pledge of Allegiance.

"See you at breakfast . . . pancakes and bacon!" Marjorie called cheerfully as Butter bounded behind her back to the Mess. The woman had an inhuman supply of energy. Southpoint didn't have cows, but if it had, I could picture Marjorie rising and shining at four a.m. to milk them for fresh cream to make butter for our pancakes.

At Southpoint we ate family-style at long wooden tables (although whose family it was styled after I didn't know, because it certainly wasn't mine). That morning it was both fun and a little strange to take a seat at the head of the table instead of on one of the low benches where the campers sat shoulder to shoulder.

At our first counselor meeting I'd volunteered to handle table assignments and had used my newfound power to put Katie Bell at my table the first week. Good thing, because I was almost literally dying to fill her in on the night before. As soon as the cowbell that signalled chow time was rung, I grabbed her across the table and whispered that she was never going to believe what went on out at the riflery range at night.

Katie Bell was mystified. She needed details, and I was more than happy to pore over the really important ones—for example, what brand of dip he used (the importance of this detail escaped me, as I thought dipping was generally gross, but Katie Bell figured he was a Skoal man), and more critically, how close, in millimeters, Ransome's knee had been to mine at the closest point of the night.

"Hel," Katie Bell gasped. "That's like, huge!" Katie Bell had a problem with whispering. She couldn't.

"What's huge?" a camper asked.

"Nothing," we both answered quickly, and luckily the camper returned, untroubled, to her stack of syrup-drenched pancakes.

"You think?" I wondered, turning back to Katie Bell. I was less confident in the morning light that the electricity I'd felt between Ransome and me wasn't imagined.

"Yes." Katie Bell gave me a look that said her opinion on the matter was to be trusted. Of course it was the answer I wanted, so I took it.

Running my life past Katie Bell over bacon—even if I was seated at the head of the table now—felt normal. But it was after breakfast that the usual camp routine skidded to a halt and took a left.

When First Call blew, the campers tramped down

to the Bowl for Morning Gathering. For the first time ever, I didn't go with them. Instead I blared music in the empty cabin and leisurely made my bed. I folded the sweatshirt and shorts I'd worn to breakfast, placing them back in my trunk in the "slightly worn" pile, and wriggled into a bathing suit.

Mornings at Southpoint meant scheduled activities with your "fish group"—age groups named after fish, smallest (Minnows) to largest (Sharks). As the lowest on the counselor totem pole, JCs got stuck teaching the activities that involved dehydrating on the athletic fields, moldering in Ye Olde Crafts Shoppe, or leading some ill-defined activity that required a lot of creativity and usually elicited little enthusiasm. Thus, my friend and fellow JC Lauren had been stuck with field hockey, Lila with crafts, Abby with leadership (i.e., trust walks), and Megan with art, which usually devolved into nail-painting and magazine reading.

I, on the other hand, had lucked out. After reading in one of her parenting books that offspring of divorced parents sometimes lack the work ethic of their co-parented counterparts, my mom had cut off my allowance for the past two summers, leaving me no choice for spending money but to babysit for the Stanley twins next door. Mrs. Stanley had insisted I get lifeguard certification before I could take her little darlings to the pool. I'd griped then, but the certification had paid off. With most of the other certified counselors on the boating dock, I'd gotten a coveted place on the swim dock with Winn and Sarah.

As I strolled out to the dock that day—instead of to Morning Gathering with Katie Bell—it felt slightly wrong, like ditching class.

Winn and Sarah were already there. They'd lugged a busted old stereo from the craft shop to the lifeguard stand, and the music carried over the lake.

At the edge of the dock I kicked off my flip-flops and stood hesitantly, wrapped in an oversize beach towel, next to Sarah and Winn. They were already stretched out on their towels, lithe bodies glistening with carrot oil. I felt dumpy. Somewhere in my mind I knew I wasn't. But that part of my mind was being suffocated by the part that had eaten four pieces of bacon at breakfast.

"*Hola,*" Winn said lazily, her eyes closed behind her sunglasses.

As I dropped my towel, I was acutely aware of Winn's taut stomach. I was tall with legs I could admit were better than average and a butt that wasn't too bad either. So I had that going for me. But I loathed the doughnut of pudge that bulged around my belly button, and the muffin top my friends and mother swore they couldn't see, but which I could actually *feel* spilling over my jeans. I was my own bakery display.

Quickly, I spread my towel next to Winn's and lay down so that the doughnut melted into the rest of my stomach. If only I could lie like this all summer.

Winn raised herself on her elbows and glanced over at me. "Ugh, I hate you. You're so tan," she said before collapsing back on her towel.

"Uh, thanks," I said. Normally I shrugged off compliments, but this one was true. Another perk of babysitting for the Stanleys. "So, which group has swimming first?"

"The Sharks," Sarah answered.

I was glad. Katie Bell was a Shark.

Content, I soaked in the sun until the peaceful calm of the lake was broken by the sound of the bugle announcing first activity.

Soon the Sharks were lined up at the edge of the dock. We stood from our towels and waited as the girls counted off—a safety precaution—before stepping onto the grayed wood.

"Okay." Winn clapped once, the sound echoing on the water, and grinned broadly. "Y'all know the drill!" She climbed the rusted rungs of the lifeguard stand and blew a shrill blast on her whistle.

Every camper, every summer, had to take a swimming

test before she could participate in any water activities. From the end of the dock by the lifeguard stand to the floating dock and back was not exactly a marathon. The test was almost silly, especially for the older girls, but required.

The Sharks dropped their towels and shorts and stood, toes curled over the edge of the dock, contemplating the freezing water below them. A few dove straight in, emerging with ear-piercing shrieks. Two girls, Amanda and Molly, held hands and unleashed a massive duel cannonball that sprayed those of us on the dock. As soon as they were in, they all started toward the floating dock.

All except Katie Bell, who shuffled over and plopped down next to me.

"So how's your first activity as a counselor?" she asked, pulling her knees under her chin.

"Good. You missed a spot." I wiped a smear of sunblock from her jawline. Katie Bell had to apply SPF 50 about six times a day at camp.

"I see they entrusted you with a whistle. That must be terribly exciting." She nodded at the cheap plastic thing in my hand.

I swung the whistle around my finger. "It saves lives."

"Safety first."

I laughed, surprised as always at how easily Katie Bell and I could pick up where we left off. We'd even made that exact promise to each other one summer. We were sitting on her bottom bunk, it was raining outside, and we were contemplating becoming blood sisters, but neither of us wanted to prick ourselves, so we settled on a long string of promises instead.

I wouldn't have been lying if I said I liked my friends at home. They were nice, and we were mostly into the same things. But they weren't the kind you trusted with the most sensitive bits of your self. I'd learned that as I'd watched them pull away after my father left, and come back only when they felt it was safe again. When we headed to college, I knew we'd lose touch.

I didn't see that happening with Katie Bell. We sat side by side on the dock in comfortable silence, watching the Sharks splash spastically across the lake. The sun felt like warm hands on my hair and shoulders.

The song on the radio changed to an old disco tune, the kind of funny, random song that you only listened to at camp, and because of that, reminded you of summer every time you heard it. Winn and Sarah started to dance on the platform of the lifeguard stand. They pulled out all the cheesy dance moves they could remember: the Lawn Mower, the Sprinkler, the Roger Rabbit. Winn did the Running Man.

"Do the Worm!" I shouted from below. Winn dropped to her stomach like she was really going to do it, sending us all into hysterics, but there wasn't enough room.

"Katie Bell," Winn called from the lifeguard stand, "you have to walk the plank too!"

Katie Bell shielded her eyes with her hand as she looked up at Winn, standing like a goddess of summer on her pedestal.

"My stomach hurts," Katie Bell called. "Female problems."

This was the excuse every camper had given at one point or another to avoid swimming. It seemed that ninety percent of Southpoint campers' menstrual cycles were attuned to the weather, because cold days saw a sharp increase in cramping. It was the only thing the counselors could report back to Fred that he wouldn't question—until the eight-year-olds overheard us and started using it as well.

"Sorry, Katie Bell," Sarah shouted this time, twirling her whistle just as I had been moments before. "Everyone has to. Dock rules."

Katie Bell heaved an exasperated sigh and looked at Sarah and Winn blankly before turning to me. "Hel," she entreated, "come on. You know I can swim. I won the freestyle at Field Day last year."

"Everyone has to, Katie Bell," Winn echoed from the lifeguard stand.

"Last time I checked," Katie Bell called, her attitude kicking in, "I don't *have* to do anything. It's camp."

"Katie Bell . . ." Winn said impatiently.

I caught Sarah rolling her eyes at Winn as she turned her back to us and faced out to the lake.

"Katie Bell," I repeated quietly, wondering why she was making this into a thing. We always had to take the swim test. It wasn't news.

She looked at me with determined disbelief. "You know I can swim."

I sighed and glanced up at Sarah and Winn, who were whispering. "I'm sorry." I shrugged helplessly. "Maybe you've forgotten since last year." Stupid joke. She wasn't buying it. "It'll only take a minute," I pleaded. "Then you can get out and sunbathe with us."

Katie Bell let out an annoyed, accusing huff and stood, dropping her towel, where it landed at my feet. She marched to the edge of the dock in front of the bench and dove off, the water barely rippling where she pierced the surface. Gracefully, she sliced through the water, quickly catching up with the last of the girls, who were doggie-paddling.

As Katie Bell tagged the floating dock and flipped to come back, the sound of a motor emerged over the teeth-chattering and talking of the landed Sharks. A boat was cruising from the center of the lake toward the swimming area. My heart skipped a beat, and I squinted to see who was driving.

Winn had come down from the lifeguard stand. She sidled up beside me. "What's her problem?" she asked, nodding at Katie Bell in the water. She seemed less irritated than perplexed.

I'd long ago accepted Katie Bell's quick temper. It was part of what made Katie Bell Katie Bell. But for others, I knew it could be jarring. "Don't worry," I sighed. "That's just Katie Bell. She hates to be told what to do."

"Yeah," Winn said, but she wasn't really listening, because now she was also peering out at the motorboat with an unreadable expression on her face.

To my half-blind eyes, the driver of the boat was just a brown figure in long swim trunks and no shirt. I assumed that it was a boy, since it was topless (or at least hoped, since it was topless). He waved. Four smaller hands also shot up in greeting.

"It's Ransome," Winn said, although I hadn't asked. One hand on her hip, she raised the other over her head and waved back, hand flopping on her wrist.

I wanted to wave but couldn't. My hands were glued to my sides like a toy soldier awaiting orders. Instinctively, I sucked in my stomach, as if the doughnut might miraculously liquefy and recongeal about two inches higher into a six-pack. But the boys couldn't see this far, and anyway, they'd already started their wide arc back toward Brownstone.

The boat's wake slapped at the dock.

"Show-off," Winn said, laughing.

I laughed too, but there was a sharp edge to Winn's comment that I wasn't sure what to do with. I was sure I'd misheard.

Katie Bell didn't speak to me for the rest of the activity period. As if to make a point, she stayed on the floating dock with Amanda and Molly, even though it meant drying and then having to dive into the cold lake again when it was time to go.

"Have a good day!" I called after the Sharks as they headed back to their cabins to change for the next activity period.

Katie Bell didn't answer, but I wasn't worried. I knew she would forgive me by dinnertime.

Chapter 6

The next morning had a chilly bite and a misty haze that would be gone by first activity but that seeped into your bones as you hurried to breakfast. As I shuffled down the path from the cabins to the Mess, via the Bath, the dew bled through my slippers and soaked the hem of my pajama pants. I shrunk deeper into my hooded sweatshirt.

No one had ever mistaken me for a morning person, but I'd had more trouble than usual getting out of bed that day. After Flag Raising, I'd plunged back into bed and joked with my campers from the comfort of my covers as they dressed for breakfast, made their beds, and began the rituals of daily cleaning. To pass inspection the cabin had to be swept, beds made, shoes lined up on cracks, trunks stowed under beds, and trash emptied. Fred ran a tight ship.

At the first breakfast bugle I'd finally dragged myself from the bed and shooed my girls out the door to the Mess. So I was perplexed when I got to the Bath to find Ruby on her tiptoes in front of one of the old spotted mirrors. Her nose was inches from the glass, and she seemed to be staring intently at her chin.

"Ruby, what are you doing?" I asked, drawing a hand from my pocket to push the hood from my head. "You're supposed to be lined up before Soupy blows."

Ruby spun around to face me. The look on her face was pained—at first, I thought, from the scolding tone of my voice.

I took a few consoling steps toward her. "Ruby, what's wrong?"

Her lip trembled slightly, but she pulled herself taller, determined not to cry. "I have spider eggs in my chin," she pronounced, as if handing down her own death sentence.

I knelt down on the wet concrete floor and examined the red spot on her chin where Ruby was pointing.

"Spider eggs?" I repeated.

"Yes," she replied, this time unable to keep her eyes from filling with tears. "A spider bit me in my sleep, and Melanie told me that means the mommy spider laid her eggs in my chin, and they're going to hatch, and a million baby spiders are gonna come out, just like in *Charlotte's Web*," she whimpered.

I pulled her into a hug and pressed my lips together hard, trying not to laugh. "Oh, Ruby," I said. "Melanie wasn't telling you the truth."

But Ruby was now wailing in my arms. "Ruby, it's okay." I smoothed her tangled ringlets. "I've gotten plenty of spider bites at camp before. You're not gonna hatch baby spiders. Melanie wasn't telling you the truth."

"Why?" She pulled back, her bottom lip poking out and her eyes confused.

"She was probably just joking."

"Why?" Ruby asked again.

Why did little girls tease each other and say untrue things? Why did big girls? It was just part of growing up, I guessed—a bonding ritual that either cemented or dissolved friendships. It was just what girls did. Even at summer camp.

"I don't know," I answered honestly.

Ruby pondered this for a second, pulling in great sucking breaths as she tried to stop crying. She pushed her palms into her eyes, wiping away the tears, and looked at me square in the face. "Well, I'm gonna joke her back," she said with determination, and took off running toward the Mess.

I laughed and grabbed my toothbrush from my

locker. As I brushed, I appraised my own face in the spotted mirror and discovered I also had a red dot on my chin. Only mine wasn't Charlotte's nest; it was a zit. Lovely. I never broke out. Finally, I thought, I had a reason to look good at camp, and my skin had chosen to freak out on me.

From the Mansion, Fred squeaked out a tinny rendition of Soupy, and I heard the Mess's screen door open and slam as hungry campers filed in. If I didn't hustle, my table would find themselves without a counselor. I quickly spit blue foam into the cracked porcelain sink, threw my toothbrush back into my locker, and pulled the skin on my chin taut for one last inspection of my zit before running in my squishy slippers to a breakfast of hot oatmeal and—another perk of being a counselor—weak coffee.

It was announced at lunch the following day that the annual Counselor vs. Cubby soccer game would take place that afternoon in Death Valley, our nickname for the scorched athletic fields past the barn. After rest hour, the whole camp gathered. On one side of the field, the counselors assembled in green Southpoint T-shirts. On the other side, in white, the cubbies circled up, strategizing how to end the counselors' three-year winning streak.

Marjorie was our referee. When she blew her whistle to start the game, I knew my plan: run around *pretending* to be interested in getting the ball, but always make sure someone else reaches it first. It was a strategy that had earned me a consistent B+ in gym class. Despite my considerable height, or maybe because of it, I'd never been the best soccer player—or any player, for that matter. I was about as good at sports as a one-armed sloth. Or so said Katie Bell.

My plan worked like a charm for the first half. By simply refraining from any action that required actual contact with the ball, I liked to think I led the counselors to our 3–1 halftime lead. Once the second half started, however, I quickly realized I had bigger problems, like keeping my pants on.

Caroline kicked the ball in my general direction. I feigned a half-assed run to it and was nearly there (safely preceded by a much more competent teammate), when I suddenly felt a warm breeze where my shorts had just been. I'd been shanked.

The campers on the sidelines howled as I whirled around to find Katie Bell running back to her side of the field, hands raised for high fives from her hooting and whistling teammates.

Yanking up my shorts, I shouted, "I know you did *not* just do that, Katie Bell!"

"Of course not," she called, putting on her best innocent-until-proven-guilty face.

"You realize I have to retaliate." From the sidelines, the campers cheered.

"Bring it!" cubby Amanda shouted.

"Oh, it's bein' broughten!" I replied, swiveling my neck in my best cheerleader-with-a-bootay-and-an-attitude-to-match impersonation. There was now a second—and much more important—game on the field.

Marjorie called off-sides in the real one, which by now had moved to the opposite goal. Breathless and laughing, Winn jogged up next to me.

"Nice granny panties," she joked.

"Thank you. My grandmother actually gave them to me."

"So you wanna get Katie Bell back?"

I was riled up, sweaty and thirsty and wanting to see some freckled Bell butt. "Um, does a Brownie crap in the woods?" I answered.

Winn laughed. "All right," she said, eyeing the field.

Katie Bell was in the middle of a skirmish with two counselors, all kicking each other for the ball.

"When she comes back down here," said Winn, "you come at her from one side, and I'll strike from the other. She won't even see me coming."

"Sounds like a plan."

We did a two-person hands-in and break.

It took two more counselor shots on goal before the ball came back to our end of the field. Perfectly, Katie Bell was leading the charge. A much more coordinated player than I, she dribbled the ball between her feet and, when she saw me coming for her, quickly passed it to another cubby. With her eyes glued on me as I clumsily rushed her, Katie Bell clutched at the waist of her shorts and nimbly sidestepped me one way and then the other. What she didn't know was that this was a two-pronged attack. As Katie Bell slithered to elude my reach, Winn grabbed her shorts from behind and yanked down hard. Katie Bell's navy running shorts puddled around her ankles. Revenge was sweet.

The campers erupted again, jumping to their feet. Katie Bell's already flushed face took on a magenta shade. She spun around to find it was Winn who had taken her down. Laughing, Winn and I high-fived each other.

"Who's a big kid now!" I taunted, getting in Katie Bell's face and beating my chest like I was some kind of trash-talking pro basketball player.

She pursed her lips. "Oh, yeah?" she retorted, cocking her head and raising an eyebrow. "I didn't need those to play anyway. I'm just gonna *beat* your pants off!"

Katie Bell gingerly stepped out of her shorts, ran to

the sidelines waving them in a circle above her head, and deposited them with the cheering campers.

In true Katie Bell fashion, she played the rest of the game in a T-shirt, underwear, and tennis shoes. Maybe it was her team's good luck charm, because when Marjorie blew the whistle to end the game, the cubbies had pulled ahead, 3 – 4. They screamed and jumped up and down as a camper ran out to give Katie Bell her shorts. She did a victory lap around the field, waving them above her head like a checkered flag.

Out of breath from running and laughing, the counselors and cubbies met in the center of the field. We all hugged and clapped each other on the back, and I picked up a now-fully-clothed Katie Bell to spin her around on my back like a rag doll.

Then the counselors formed a huddle to give the winners their big prize: "Two, four, six, eight!" we chanted. "Who do we appreciate? Cubbies, cubbies, cubbies! Three, five, seven, nine! Who do we think is mighty fine? Cubbies, cubbies, cubbies!"

When we were done, Katie Bell stretched on her tiptoes to hook her arm around my neck. I slung my arm around her shoulders, and together we were swept along with the flow of campers and counselors trickling from Death Valley to the cabins.

After the game there was a long free period before

dinner. Katie Bell would probably spend hers at the barn, and I had to change into my bathing suit and get to the swim dock. But for now, we'd just enjoy the moment.

"Good game," said Katie Bell, a smile twitching at the corners of her mouth.

I laughed. "Yeah. Good game." It occurred to me then that this was the first time all week it had felt like we were on the same team.

Dinner was always the loudest meal of the day. Activities were over, and speculation on what the night's Evening Gathering would be circulated table to table. Evening Gatherings were a surprise closely guarded by the counselors. Would it be casino night, the counselor show, Miss Fat Chance, cabin skits, a bonfire and ghost story? Only the counselors knew until the big reveal at dinner, and the campers' anticipation ensured the liveliness of our evening meal. The sound was now reaching an almost deafening crescendo.

"Please pass the baked beans," Ruby piped as loud as she could above the din.

From the other end of the table, a large steaming bowl of baked beans was passed hand to hand to Ruby. Camp food was hearty, delicious, and should have been hugely fattening. Our husband-and-wife cooks, Tee and Rosie, had been with Fred's family since he was a little boy. They were of the old-school tradition that worshipped the holy trinity of butter, bacon, and refined carbs. There was no such thing as dieting at camp, but we never seemed to gain weight. It was a miracle worthy of Vatican review.

Ruby spooned three heaping mounds of the bubbling brown beans onto her plate, next to her barbecued chicken and corn bread. She had declined broccoli even after Katie Bell made an elaborate, if transparent, show of how good it tasted and threatened that Ruby had better eat her vegetables or she'd never get big boobs.

"Is that why you don't have big boobs?" Ruby had asked in a spasm of giggles.

"Valid point," Katie Bell had observed.

She now turned to me, her elbows propped on the table. "So what's Evening Gathering tonight?" she asked as she chewed.

"Eww, Katie Bell, I can see the food in your mouth."

"What, this?" Katie Bell opened her mouth so wide I could see the broccoli stuck in her molars.

"Gross!"

Katie Bell laughed. "Sorry. So what's for Evening Gathering?" she repeated, trying to whisper.

I shushed her, gesturing toward Ruby and the other campers at the table. Leaning over, I cupped my hands over her ear. "Lip synch," I whispered.

She brightened. Lip synch had always been one of our favorites. My job was picking the song and carefully transcribing the lyrics for us to memorize. Katie Bell was in charge of choreography and costumes, which meant raiding our cabinmates' trunks for the most outrageous outfits she could find—the tighter and more sparkly the better. Polyester always went over well.

"What song are we gonna do?" she asked.

Ruby was watching us, listening. "Are you talking about Evening Gathering?" she asked, with the tiniest hint of a lisp.

"Nope," Katie Bell answered quickly. "We were just talking about a camp mix we're making."

"Oh," Ruby said, disappointed. She turned her attention back to one of her new friends at the table.

"Actually . . ." I hesitated as I leaned in, "I think the counselors are doing a song together."

In fact, I knew we were. Lizbeth had organized it. We'd come up with the song, Aretha Franklin's version of "Respect," and all the choreography on the dock during rest hour.

"Oh." Katie Bell gave a short, indifferent shrug. "Okay. That's fine. Amanda and Molly had already mentioned something to me anyway. Lizbeth told them too. I actually knew. I just forgot."

I nodded like I believed her, but before I could say I

was sorry or offer to do a song with her too, Winn had appeared at the table.

"Scooch," she announced, gesturing for Katie Bell to slide down the bench and make room for her to sit next to me. "What's up?"

"Stacking, soon," I said, stating the obvious. The meal was almost over, and we had to clear our plates before dessert was brought out.

"Oh my God, Hel." Winn laughed. "You have to remind me to tell you later what Peyton Smith said in my cabin today."

Peyton was one of our more "special" campers. She stuck to herself but still seemed to still love camp. She came every year and brought her entire collection of American Girl dolls. Her favorites she took everywhere with her, even to activities.

"What?" I asked, already laughing too.

"I'll tell you later," she promised. "Also"—Winn lowered her voice and turned her back to Katie Bell and the rest of the table—"I just wanted to tell you we're going out to the range tonight."

"Great! I'm there."

"Okay, cool." Winn stood. "Thanks," she said, patting Katie Bell's shoulder. "You can have your seat back." Winn leaned over and plucked a hunk of corn bread from Katie Bell's plate. "Mmmm." She drew her mouth into a closed smile, shrugging her eyebrows, and headed back to her table.

"What was that about?" Katie Bell asked, watching Winn cross the crowded dining room.

I leaned in with my hand at her ear and whispered so low Katie Bell held her breath to hear me.

"Are you gonna go?" she asked.

"Yeah." I nodded. Why wouldn't I, I wondered. Ransome would be there.

"You have to report back. Everything."

"I did last time, didn't I?"

"Who's stacking, Helena?" a camper called down to me from the middle of the table.

I looked at Katie Bell. "I promise I'll tell you everything," I said in a low voice. Then I looked at Pookie, who sat at the other end of the table. She shrugged. It was up to me.

"You are, Lindsay!" I replied enthusiastically. "Thanks!"

Lindsay groaned but dutifully obeyed as the other girls gladly passed their plates. No one escaped stacking.

No one except the counselors. Drunk on my power, I passed my plate to Lindsay and crunched on the last piece of ice stuck at the bottom of my cup.

Fred tapped on the cowbell above his table to call us to order. He would be announcing the lip synch, and the girls would soon be a tsunami of excitement, forming groups and picking songs. But I had other things to be excited about. The evening gathering I was concerned with was the one that would happen at the riflery range after Taps.

As we trooped after Evening Gathering from the Bowl to the Bath, Katie Bell was quiet. Katie Bell, Amanda, and Molly had won the lip synch with a rousing rendition of "It's in His Kiss," but I could tell for Katie Bell the win was lost behind something else she was working over in her head like a worry bead.

We brushed our teeth in silence, surrounded by a swarm of campers splashing water and loudly singing the refrain. I had to spit over the head of a camper.

Cold and damp, we left the Bath and started slowly up the hill to the cabins. But Katie Bell stopped in the pool of light beneath the floodlight that lit the way for campers who had to pee in the middle of the night.

"Hey," she said suddenly, turning to face me. Her hands were shoved deep in the pockets of her jeans. "Why wouldn't Winn say it in front of me?"

"Huh?"

"Why did Winn hide that from me—about the riflery range—at dinner?"

I knew, as well as Katie Bell, why Winn hadn't said it in front of her, why she had literally turned her back as she told me. Because Katie Bell was a camper, and I was a counselor. Because counselors hid those things from campers. Because they were afraid of getting in trouble.

"She probably just didn't want anyone to hear," I said, brushing it off. "Don't worry about it."

"I'm not *worried* about it," Katie Bell said defensively. "I just think it's weird, that's all. It's kind of rude." She dug her tennis shoe into the grass and swung her camping chair across her shoulder.

Suddenly Katie Bell's face turned hard, and there was an arm around my shoulder. It was Winn. Her hoodie was pulled over her blond hair, and the angle of the floodlight cast dark shadows on her face, giving her a sinister look, like the killer in one of Fred's scarier ghost stories.

"Hey," she said cheerily, throwing back her hood and restoring her usually more angelic appearance. "Good job, Katie Bell. Y'all were hilarious. Never would have thought you could pull off drag."

Katie Bell had played the song's love interest—a Brownie.

"Maybe you can teach drama next year?" Winn joked.

"Maybe," Katie Bell replied humorlessly.

Winn's smile froze, her eyebrows raised quizzically

at Katie Bell's shortness. "O-kay," she said.

A couple of campers passed through the circle of light with their arms around each other's shoulders, laughing as they slogged up the hill. It was a stark contrast to the arctic chill currently emanating from Winn and Katie Bell.

"Anyway . . ." Winn continued, looking at me, "I'll see you later, Helena?"

She said this deliberately, with a wink in her voice, not knowing Katie Bell already knew what she was trying to say without saying it. I could feel Katie Bell bristle beside me.

"Yeah." I made my voice as colorless and neutral as possible. "I'll meet y'all at the Mess after Taps," I said quickly.

Winn nodded and jogged off to catch up with Lizbeth.

"I think I need a Tums," Katie Bell said suddenly.

"Why?" I asked, confused.

"Must be the baked beans. I'm gonna run down to the Mansion." It wasn't exactly a strange thing to do. A lot of us got heartburn from Rosie and Tee's cooking. Tums were handed out like after-dinner mints at the infirmary.

"Okay." I shrugged. "Well, do you want me to come get you later? After . . ."

"Sure," she answered. "Yeah. Come wake me up, definitely. Have fun."

"All right. Feel better," I said, but it was to the back of her sweatshirt. She had already turned to walk quickly to the Mansion.

"Shhhhhh!"

Six of us were creeping along the path that led from the riflery range to the lake and circled around to the swim dock. The rest of the counselors at the range had bailed. We tiptoed single file. All I could see was Winn's back shaking with the giggles in front of me.

"Shhhh," Sarah whispered again, laughing even as she scolded us. "Sound carries over water!"

Winn turned to fake a serious face. In front of us, Buzz and another Brownie, Nate, led on. Behind me, Ransome accidentally stepped on the heel of my flip-flop.

"Sorry," he whispered.

"It's okay," I whispered back.

Finally, the trail opened onto the main path to the lake. Crouching low, we snuck across the clearing and down to the dock. The water stretched out peacefully before us.

Ransome had made good on his threat: we were going skinny-dipping.

"I can't believe we're doing this," I murmured, watching nervously as everyone started to remove their shoes.

Ransome, standing beside me with a boot in his hand, paused. "Are you scared?" he asked. As far as I could tell, he wasn't teasing; he was serious. The concern was sweet.

And yes, I *was* scared. The thought of being naked in a big dark lake with the fish and snakes I was sure lived there . . . yeah, it kinda scared me. Wasn't this how *Jaws* started? But what freaked me out more was the thought of shucking my clothes and standing buck naked in front of Ransome and the other Brownies, even if for only a second.

My pulse quickened, the blood beating through my head and chest, as I realized Ransome would be naked too. Nothing between us but moonlight and water. Suddenly the idea that had seemed so carefree and fun at the riflery range was a lot more fraught with anxiety than I'd imagined.

Then again, wasn't this exactly the kind of scene I'd always fantasized about? A playful, quickly-turned-seductive moonlit moment with Ransome? It occurred to me maybe I should just count my blessings and strip—like ripping off a Band-Aid.

Ransome had dropped his pants to reveal a pair of blue-striped boxers, but he saw I hadn't moved an inch, had barely breathed. "You don't have to get in if you don't want to," he reassured me. "We won't make fun of you—or we might, but it will pass."

"No, I'm not scared," I answered, even though that had been the question two minutes ago.

He smiled.

I realized everyone else around me was almost full monty. Slowly, I slipped off my flip-flops and pulled my shirt over my head, holding it in front of me for just a few more milliseconds of privacy.

"Geronimo!" Buzz took a running leap off the dock and landed in a perfect cannonball. The water sprayed up around him.

"Buzz!" Nate hissed. "You're gonna get us caught, dumbass. Be quiet!"

Buzz shook the water from his hair, like a golden retriever. Below the surface, his body was a pale, moving blur. I was relieved I couldn't make out more.

Suddenly, I startled as two more white streaks blurred past me. Winn and Sarah. They dropped into the water as straight as pencils to avoid a loud splash. When they emerged, they were gasping and laughing.

"Is it cold?" I asked.

"Um, yeah," Winn confirmed, her teeth chattering.

As Nate turned to climb casually down the dock ladder, my eyes must have widened to the size of dinner plates. Full frontal, like it was nothing at all. I realized I was staring and quickly looked away.

No one but Ransome and me were on the dock now. The others in the water swam out toward the floating dock, all keeping a safe distance from each other. At one point, Buzz came toward Sarah as if he was going to dunk her, but I heard her splash and, laughing, threaten bodily harm if he got any closer.

I was down to my underwear and bra, and saying a silent prayer that I hadn't worn my granny panties that day. Ransome stood in his boxers watching the others from the dock. He looked at me, and my cheeks burned. I wanted to shield myself with my hands, cover my doughnut, obscure my love handles from the world. He didn't seem to notice. Gratefully, he was looking me in the eyes.

"You first," I said, hoping to sound like a confident sex kitten instead of a squeaky, aquaphobic prude.

Ransome laughed. "Okay. But you're following me. . . ."

I nodded. Ransome stood at the edge of the dock, directly in front of me to spare me a crotch shot, and dropped his boxers around his ankles. I almost laughed out loud. His butt looked like two little white apples in the moonlight. I had a weird impulse—where I wasn't sure I could control the urge to grab it.

Quickly, he climbed down the ladder and was soon paddling in front of the dock. He looked up at me. "Your turn."

"Fine. But you have to turn around."

"That's no fun." I could see the crooked tooth in his grin.

I crossed my arms over my chest, suppressing a smile, and raised an eyebrow.

"Okay, okay." He paddled around so that he was looking out across the lake.

The others were preoccupied watching nude Nate try to climb onto the floating dock without scratching anything valuable. In a hurry, I stripped out of my underwear and bra, dropping them on the dock in a pile with my other clothes, and slid into the water noiselessly.

It was so cold it almost knocked the wind out of me. I shivered as the hairs on my legs stood at attention. So much for shaving.

"Boo," I said, swimming up behind Ransome.

He turned, treading water. "It's not so bad, see?" he said in breaths clipped by the freezing water.

"No, it's not," I agreed. The water rushed around my legs and stomach and arms as I kicked. I was acutely aware of just how close—and how naked—Ransome was in the water.

We looked at each other for a few seconds, both of

us pawing at the water, until I laughed uncomfortably, not knowing what other reaction to have.

Ransome slapped at the water, sending a spray into my face. "What are you laughing at?" he asked.

"Nothing!" I answered honestly.

He splashed me again. I spluttered. "Stop!" I laughed and splashed back.

We were circling around each other in a splashing fight, which was as playful as it could be considering we had to be quiet, when I heard Winn's and Sarah's voices. They had swum back closer to the dock now.

"Who is that?" Winn asked urgently.

"What are they doing?" Sarah asked at the same time.

Winn gasped, and suddenly they were both swimming frantically for the dock. Terrified, I turned to see what—or who—they were looking at, but all I could make out were a few dark figures moving around the dock.

Then it hit me like a brick. It was other Brownies, and they were taking our clothes!

I raced behind Winn and Sarah to the ladder, but by the time we got there it was too late. Our clothes were gone.

A furious Winn spun in the water to glare at the three offenders still in the lake. Nate, Buzz, and Ransome were all laughing.

"You assholes!" Winn hissed. She wanted to scream, but she knew if she did, Fred or the campers would hear us.

"You stole our clothes?" Sarah asked, stating the obvious.

I continued to tread water and look dumbly between the guys and the girls, unsure of what to do. *Shit*, I thought. They'd made the first strike. Shit. We were naked, at least fifty yards from our cabins, and we had no clothes. Shit. I hoped, at least, the boys had had the chivalry to leave our shoes.

Buzz was still cracking up. "Ha-ha. Suckas!"

"You *do* know this is not the beginning of some porny lesbian-camp fantasy, right, Buzz?" Winn asked.

"It can if you want it to be," he said lasciviously.

Sarah muttered a disgusted "Ugh," and the three of us huddled as close as we could in a circle without touching each other.

"All right," Winn said, trying to maintain calm. "Here's what we're gonna do. I'm gonna take one of their shirts and run up to my cabin and get us some towels. . . . Shit! I can't believe we fell for this!"

Internally, I heaved a huge sigh of relief that I wouldn't be running bare-assed back to the cabins, dripping like a pale, wet joke.

Winn shot the boys one more withering glare before climbing from the lake and grabbing the closest shirt she could find, which happened to be Ransome's. She pulled the flannel shirt over her head. It hung just below her butt. I was glad, but in a weird way, slighty jealous.

"I'll be right back," Winn grumbled. She took off running—something we were never supposed to do on the docks—toward the cabins. I could hear her footfalls retreat down the path.

Sarah and I turned to the guys, who were watching us, greatly amused.

"Y'all come here often?" joked Buzz.

Sarah sneered. "Nice, Buzz."

"We got you good, though, right?" said Nate.

"Oh, it's *on*," replied Sarah, looking to me for backup.

"I hope you know what you've gotten yourself into." I leveled my most menacing stare at Ransome.

He returned it with a lopsided smile. "I think so," he said, not breaking my gaze. I wasn't sure he was talking about the prank war anymore.

It felt like an eternity before Winn returned, but the guys didn't leave until we were safely out of the water and wrapped in our towels.

"Ranny will bring your clothes back tomorrow," Buzz assured, still beaming proudly as we quicky stole off the dock and up the path to our cabins.

"We'll be looking forward to it," Winn shot sarcastically over her shoulder.

The boys laughed, and we disappeared into the darkness of the trees, thoroughly beaten but newly determined. The other counselors would hear about this. It was time to mobilize.

"Katie Bell," I whispered. "Katie Bell."

I was panting from the run up to the cabins and afraid the sound of my breathing might wake the whole cabin. I had even left my shoes at the door to avoid creaking on the old wooden floor.

"Katie Bell." I shook her gently. Like me, Katie Bell was a champion sleeper.

I shook her harder. "Katie Bell," I whispered more impatiently this time.

"Huh?" She stirred. "What?" She raised her disheveled head and looked at me with heavy-lidded eyes that popped open in alarm as she came to.

"Shhh." I laughed. "It's me. It's Hel. Come on, I have to tell you about tonight."

Katie Bell's brain finally focused. Nodding, she pushed her covers aside and yawned. Her ponytail was matted against her head, half of it pushed up and looking like a bad hairpiece, and the other half falling out of its rubber band. I gestured with my head at the door, and Katie Bell grabbed her bathrobe off a nail and followed me out to "our spot" at the softball diamond behind the cabins. It was our unspoken rule that if one of us couldn't sleep, she would wake the other up to come talk on the bleachers. It was usually me who did the waking. Katie Bell and I had spent several nights out there the summer my parents split, and the following summer when Katie Bell first got her period.

She padded quietly behind me now through the rows of dark cabins. We didn't speak until we were both seated on the metal bleachers. They were so cold they felt wet. I was glad I had stopped quickly at my cabin to trade Winn's towel for flannel pajama pants and a long-sleeve T-shirt before retrieving Katie Bell.

"Sooo," she said when we were surrounded by nothing but field and pine trees. Her hands were sandwiched between her knees for warmth. She was awake, and all ears. "What happened?"

"It was awesome . . . we went skinny-dipping . . . I saw Ransome naked, Katie Bell . . . and they took our clothes!" It all came rushing out in one breath. My body was buzzing with excitement, from my feet to my fingertips—one long twisted rope of kinetic energy.

"Skinny-dipping?"

I nodded, my eyes mirroring hers and growing wide.

"Like, naked?" she asked.

"Yeah." I laughed. "What other way do you do it?"

"I don't know . . . It's just that . . . *You*? Skinny-dipping?"

Katie Bell knew I wasn't exactly an exhibitionist. She might have grown up running around naked and wild in the country, but in my house, they were called "private parts" for a reason. Last summer was the first I would even take my bathing suit off in the showers. Still, her tone bugged me.

"Yeah," I said again. "Me. Skinny-dipping . . . with Ransome. Did you hear that part?"

She raised an eyebrow. "Just Ransome?"

"No," I said, wishing she would just understand. "Remember how I told you about last time at the riflery range? Ransome said he was going to take me skinny-dipping for the first time—or said we were all gonna go before camp was over—whatever. You remember?" Katie Bell nodded. "Well, we did it!" I laughed again. "Me, Winn, Sarah, Buzz, Nate, and Ransome."

"And you saw him naked?" Katie Bell asked, crossing her arms against the chilly mountain air.

"Yes! Well, actually I just saw his butt."

"Did he see *you* naked?"

"No! I made him turn around in the water while I

got in . . . but then—oh my God, Katie Bell, it was so embarrassing—some of the other Brownies snuck out to the dock and stole our clothes!"

Katie Bell was confused. "All of your clothes? The guys' too?"

"No, just Winn's and mine and Sarah's. Winn had to run up to the cabins in Ransome's shirt to grab us towels."

As I said it, I couldn't believe it had all actually happened.

"That's crazy," Katie Bell agreed, with a small chuckle.

"I know. I guess the prank war's on. But the campers can't know about this one," I added quickly. "Just the counselors—and you, of course."

"Of course." Katie Bell nodded. There was a moment of silence. It was awkward, but I couldn't put my finger on why.

I almost didn't say it, but then I had to. "Katie Bell, I think . . ." I hesitated. "I think Ransome was flirting with me tonight."

"Really?" Katie Bell asked. One of her eyebrows went north. She was finally getting as excited as I thought she would have been when we started this conversation.

I crinkled my nose and shrugged. "Yeah. At least, I think so. . . ."

There was something about Ransome that was very self-contained. I could tell he wasn't one of those guys like Buzz, who prodded and teased to get your attention, like the little boy pulling pigtails on the playground. He hadn't taken the small opportunities that I know had been there to touch my arm or my leg or to whisper in my ear. Still, I'd felt something between us tonight, the same electric current I'd felt the first night at the riflery range. I wondered if anyone else had noticed, if it was obvious . . . or if it was nothing more than a crush's deluded imagination.

"Hel, that's awesome," said Katie Bell. In the moonlight her pale face was almost luminous. "You're totally gonna hook up with him."

"It's just so crazy," I said, replaying the night in my head, unable to let it go. As if I stopped thinking or talking about it, the moment would cease to exist. "All these things go on that we never knew about, you know? It's like camp—grown up."

Katie Bell nodded in agreement but seemed distracted, looking over my shoulder at the dark shapes of the cabins hunkered to the ground under the weight of the night sky.

It was late. I groaned. "I'm gonna be so freaking tired tomorrow."

"Yeah, I'm freezing. I gotta go back to bed, Helena."

"Okay," I sighed, hopping off the bleachers.

We parted at the door to Katie Bell's cabin. "Good night," I called in a whisper.

Hunched against the cold, she paused in the doorway as if she was going to say something. But she just said "'Night" and disappeared into the shadows.

As I walked between the cabins, I sighed and tipped back my head to search the sky. The stars had disappeared behind a gauzy cover of clouds. It was strange being the only person outside the cabins at night—scary and exhilarating, completely exposed and totally free.

Tattoo

The sweet tang of rotting hay tickles my nose, threatening to make me sneeze. Soft exhalations and the stamping of hooves come from the stalls. Saddles and halters, reins and leads, so many leather straps, burnished black-brown.

Shovels are propped against the wall, not where they're supposed to be—the stable girls knew that but didn't care when they ran off for free time. They also missed a trail of manure, brown turned black and hard, covered by drunk flies. The smell is pungent but not exactly unpleasant. This is a barn, after all.

In her stall, a horse whinnies and paces from wall to wall, impatient for a rider. One will come soon enough, and then she'll shake her head against the reins, wanting to canter when she trots, and trot when she canters. But now, as she whinnies, motes of dust dance in shafts of sunlight that pierce through the old boards, and the sun begins to set.

Chapter 7

Five girls hovered around one trunk in the middle of Winn's cabin as Winn and I watched the feeding frenzy from her bed. The owner of the trunk, a camper named Hannah, was apparently the only one who had come prepared for a dance. It was therefore her duty to outfit her entire cabin. That's just what sisters did.

"I don't know why I didn't pack any cute clothes," a fry named Thea lamented as she picked a striped tube top from Hannah's trunk and went to stand, pouting, before the cabin's one mirror, which had been tilted to offer a full body shot. "Will horizontal stripes make me look fat?"

Thea resembled a beanpole and couldn't have looked fat if she wore a tube top made of puffer vests.

Another girl, Jordan, rolled her eyes. "Of course

not, Thea. You've got, like, the hottest body."

Winn and I had to exchange glances and smother a laugh. Thea was eleven. If anyone thought her body was "hot," he was a certified perv. Except, I guessed, for eleven-year-olds from Brownstone, which was exactly the point at your first camp dance.

It was early Saturday evening, which meant in a couple of hours, all of Brownstone would load on to buses and drive around the tip of the lake for a cookout and dance on our tennis courts. Fred always hired the same DJ from town, who thought we still listened to 'NSync and called himself "Dr. Spin."

The day of the boys' arrival was always frantic. There was the complicated matter of finding the perfect outfit, the bigger issue of hair when there were no hair dryers because there were no electrical outlets, and, of course, important decisions regarding which boys would be danced with and which would be shunned for no other reason than that was the consensus that week. The younger girls watched the older ones for cues, and the very youngest either watched in awe or ignored everyone, wondering what all the fuss was about. They were just happy for the free time to catch frogs in the shallow creek by the footbridge or, if they were of the girly type, to play with their counselor's makeup. Which was why Ruby appeared suddenly breathless in the door of Winn's cabin as we watched Jordan consider whether a tube top did anything for Thea's "figure."

"*There* you are!" Ruby huffed, as if a search party of hounds had been combing the camp grounds. Her small hands locked around my wrist and yanked. "Come on! You said we could use your makeup before the dance."

In order to get my cabin to keep quiet at rest hour, I'd had to promise they could play with my makeup.

"All right, all right," I said, letting Ruby drag me off of Winn's bed. "I'll see you in a few?" I asked, glancing back at Winn.

"You still want an S.C. before the dance?" she confirmed, with a furtive look.

I nodded. "S.C." was Winn's code for "secret cigarette." At home I never smoked. I didn't hang out with people who did. My friends, including Katie Bell, declared smoking "gross" with squinched faces and upturned noses, but somehow in the past week, I'd kind of picked up the habit. I never asked for a cigarette, but if Winn volunteered one from her pack or asked me to go with her, I never turned her down. Her "P Funks" left a taste in my mouth like dirty socks steeped in crap, and the smell of the lotion we had to slather on afterward to cover the smell made me slightly nauseous, but the thrill of sneaking away because we were counselors and not every minute of our day was accounted for made smoking seem glamorous in a way I'd never understood before.

Having promised to meet Winn later, I let Ruby drag me by the hand back to our cabin. My makeup, which I usually kept stashed high on the shelf in my cubby, was already scattered across my bed. Beneath the shelf, a pink Tupperware trunk had been pulled up—a telltale sign of a nine-year-old snoop.

My girls were inspecting the various tubes, compacts, and bottles, like archaeological artifacts. I was surprised to find Katie Bell there too. She sat on my bed, about to apply a lip-plumping gloss to the puckered lips of my camper Abby.

"Wait—" I started to grab the applicator from Katie Bell's hand, but it was too late.

"Ow, ow, owwwww!" Abby danced in a circle, her hands flailing like two spider monkeys at her sides. Both Katie Bell and Ruby looked at me, bewildered.

"That stuff stings," I explained. "Abby, are you okay?"

She stuck out her lips in an exaggerated pout, her eyes crossing as she tried to see her own mouth. "Aw ma wips pwumpa?"

"Absolutely," I assured.

"Sorry, Abby." Katie Bell laughed, tossing the gloss back on my bed. "I didn't know Helena kept controlled substances in her makeup bag. Hey," she said, turning to me, "are you gonna help me pick out an outfit?"

Katie Bell was a self-admitted fashion victim. Workout shorts, a T-shirt, and tennis shoes were her camp uniform. Not giving a monkey's ass what you looked like was part of the beauty and point of camp. But since we'd started actually caring about dances—when we'd first realized the Brownies were more than just extras—come Saturday night, I was Katie Bell's personal stylist.

"Um, yeah," I said distractedly, but I was worried about the time. I still had to set up the refreshments table and get back to meet Winn for our S.C. before clothing check at the flagpole. We had to vet our campers' outfits for enough fabric in the appropriate places.

"Why don't you wear that cute green sundress Pookie gave you last summer?" I offered.

Katie Bell wasn't convinced. "It's too short now. Can't you tell I grew three-quarters of an inch last year? I've legally surpassed the designation of 'little person,'" she joked.

"Well, did you bring that yellow tank top?"

"Yeah, but I wore that to, like, every dance last summer," she whined, her head lolling to one side.

"I don't know, Katie Bell," I answered, my impatience showing as I straightened my bed and put the makeup back into its polka-dotted plastic pouch.

"Can't you just come look in my trunk real quick?" Katie Bell's indecision was slowly being replaced by irritation and confusion at my reluctance to help her.

I was annoyed too, but not sure why. It was a perfectly reasonable request. But the tiny gears on my watch were ticking loudly. I had to get down to the tennis courts to help Pookie with the folding tables and big orange Gatorade coolers, and then back to meet Winn.

And for some reason, I didn't want Katie Bell to know about our secret cigarettes.

"I'm sorry, Katie Bell, but I have to help with the drinks and stuff. I think you should wear the yellow tank top." I grabbed a rubber band and rolled it onto my wrist. "I have to run, but I'll see you at the dance."

"Okay," Katie Bell mumbled, obviously ticked off.

I gave her what I hoped passed for an apologetic smile and hurried out of the cabin and down the path past the Mansion to the tennis courts.

Getting back for an S.C. with Winn wasn't the only thing making me anxious. I was already on a heightened state of alert knowing Ransome would be at the dance tonight. Thinking of the last time I saw him, naked as the day he came into the world, I laughed to myself. I wondered if he would be able to read it on my face tonight as clearly as if it were stenciled in black Sharpie across my forehead: HELENA LUVS RANSOME.

I also *did* feel bad about leaving Katie Bell, but Pookie was already lugging a huge orange cooler across the tennis court by herself, so I pushed my nervousness and guilt aside and jogged to help her. Maybe an S.C. with Winn would calm me down.

Off a never-used path behind the softball diamond, there was a small outcropping of rock that was the perfect spot for two counselors to sneak away for a cigarette. Winn had shown it to me the first time she asked me to come with her, and this was where we found ourselves before the dance.

Without asking if I wanted one, she flipped open the top of her pack, revealing three rows of white filters lined up nice and neat like little tar soldiers, and held it out to me.

I slid one from the pack and fumbled with the lighter as I held the cigarette in my lips. I didn't have the smooth, practiced mannerisms that Winn did. She inhaled deeply and exhaled impressive plumes of smoke, while I took short, shallow puffs and managed to get ash everywhere.

Winn draped her arms over her tanned knees, bare

below a pair of short army-green shorts. "Thanks for coming with me," she said.

"Sure." I rubbed my foot where the rock had left an indent in my ankle, and repositioned myself so that I was sitting like Winn, feet flat on the rock and knees up.

"Sarah and Buzz are totally gonna hook up again this summer," Winn said out of the blue, picking a fleck of tobacco from her tongue.

"You think?" By now, I knew all about Sarah and Buzz's fling the year before.

"Sarah says she's not interested." Winn rolled her eyes. "But . . . come on. They're totally gonna hook up."

I'd hesitated in saying anything to Winn until now. I was afraid it would seem stupid to her, but suddenly I *had* to spill about Ransome.

"Can I tell you something?" I asked, gnawing at my lower lip.

"Sure." Her blue eyes fixed on me.

"So, I kind of have a crush on someone, and I know it's ridiculous, but . . ."

Winn's eyes lit up. "Who?!" she cried, suddenly riveted.

I smiled and held back for a second. I thought her eyes might pop out of her head from the suspense.

Finally I spit it out. "Ransome," I said, and quickly buried my head in my arms.

"Ransome?"

"Yes." I groaned. "I know it's ridiculous. He's, like, three years older and probably sees me as just this dorky JC, but I've had a crush on him since I was, like, nine."

"I think we *all* did at some point," Winn said, almost to herself.

Her statement made me feel silly rather than better. I was trying to tell her this was more than just a camper's crush now. I really liked him.

I took too big a drag on my cigarette and immediately started coughing like I was going to eject a lung.

"You okay?" Winn laughed.

Cough, cough. "Yeah." *Cough.*

"That's what you get for hittin' the hard stuff," she joked.

"What? Black lung?" I laughed.

"Yeah." She stubbed out her cigarette, already down to the filter. Mine was only halfway done, but I put it out anyway. It had already left a nasty metallic taste in my mouth.

"Shoot," Winn said, checking her watch. "We better get down there soon. Do you want some?" She held out a travel-size bottle of mango-coconut lotion that she kept in the makeup bag she used to stash her cigarettes, a lighter, and Listerine strips.

"Thanks." I let her squeeze a blob of the odorous lotion into my hands and rubbed it in between my fingers. I knew they'd still smell like burned tires, which made me wish I hadn't smoked. Would Ransome notice? I hoped my hair and clothes didn't reek too.

As we stood and brushed the dirt from the butts of our shorts, I had an uneasy feeling in the pit of my stomach that I knew wasn't just the cigarette.

"Hey, Winn . . ." I started.

"Yeah?"

In the dappled light of the woods, Winn looked really pretty. Next to her, I felt suddenly gawky. Too tall for myself.

I held my breath. "Will you promise not to tell anyone about Ransome? I mean, that I like him?"

"Yeah." She nodded as if it went without saying. "Of course."

"Thanks."

"Sure," she said, and headed for the edge of the clearing. "That's what friends are for."

From the rickety bleachers that lined one long side of the tennis courts, Winn, Lizbeth, Sarah, Pookie, and I surveyed the scene. The smell of charred hamburgers still hung like a cloud in the air. Dr. Spin was in the middle of a playlist of the Top 40 songs . . . of 2003. And we were armed with Super Soakers.

A few summers ago, Fred and Abe had decided the counselors should uphold the decorum of these mixers by spraying any couples who were dancing too close with water guns. It was a joke more than anything, as still—with the exception of the youngest girls, who unself-consciously shimmied and shook like little booty dancers in the center of the court—most of the campers refused to even mingle. The tennis nets had been taken down for the dance, but their poles provided a clear-cut boundary. On their respective sides, the girls and boys congregated in tight clusters, pretending to ignore each other as they stole furtive glances. Only when night fell would they come together and actually dance.

At the edge of the court, where determined clumps of grass cracked and poked through the pavement, I noticed Katie Bell talking with Molly and Amanda. She was wearing the yellow tank top. I felt a rush of guilt about brushing her off before.

As I watched, Katie Bell whispered in Molly's ear, and both girls glanced over their shoulders at a group of Brownstone boys before collapsing in hysterics. A weird feeling suddenly came over me. I had the impression that I was watching Katie Bell and the others on a home video. It was a moment's mental snap-shot, and I knew every time I would recall this frame of my life, this summer, I would feel just the same as I did right then. It was strange—a nostalgia for something that was still happening.

Unsettled by this feeling of being telescoped through time, I looked away from Katie Bell and focused on the conversation next to me. The tone had changed. Winn, Sarah, and Pookie were intently discussing the three Brownies scraping the grills from the cookout. Buzz was one of them, and Winn and Pookie were interrogating Sarah, as well as pumping her for information on Ben, the Brownie that Lizbeth, who had momentarily slipped away to the bathroom, liked, but who the other girls thought was kind of a dud.

I tried to pay attention, listening carefully for any-thing about Ransome. He had just disappeared into the Mess. But my attention was drawn back to Katie Bell. She and some other cubbies were snapping pictures now, taking turns making goofy or seductive faces at the camera and then eagerly checking to see if the picture was save-worthy or should be instantly erased and reshot.

When she noticed me watching her, Katie Bell asked for the camera from Molly and skipped over to the bleachers.

"Hey," she said. I listened for a hint in her voice that

she was still mad that I hadn't helped her pick out an outfit, but her earlier irritation seemed to have evaporated.

Instead, she launched into a gushing monologue. "Charlie is, like, the biggest freaking dork ever!" She glanced over her shoulder at Charlie Banks, who she herself had had a crush on just two summers before. "I can't *buhlieve* Molly kissed him last summer. Did you know that? She made out with him at the last dance last year behind the Mess. He is such a tool! He's still wearing his aviators, and it's, like, almost night-time."

For some reason, Katie Bell's excited chatter embarrassed me. Lizbeth, Sarah, and Winn were listening. And Ransome, who had come out of the Mess, was looking in our direction. A moment ago I'd been almost jealous of her. Now all I wanted was for Katie Bell to play it cool, to not be so dramatic for once, to not be such . . . a kid.

"Hel," she continued, not sensing how I was flinching inwardly at the way she drew attention to herself with her loud voice and unrestrained excitement, "let's get a picture of Hels Bells!"

Where it previously had seemed funny and even cool, the nickname now rang in my ears as glaringly immature.

Katie Bell scrambled up onto the bleachers next to me, handing her camera to Lizbeth before throwing her arm around my neck. She grinned at the camera, and I grimaced. My face was on fire as I felt Ransome watching us, my skin crawling with how much I did not want to be in this moment. As Lizbeth leaned back, counted to three, and took the photo, I pulled a taut smile across my face and tried to appear somehow more mature than my friend next to me.

"Okay!" I said brightly when the photo was taken.

"Don't you want to see it?" asked Katie Bell, retrieving the camera from Lizbeth.

"That's okay. I'm sure it's fine."

She looked at me strangely and climbed down from the bleachers. "All right." All the spunk that had just animated her voice had drained out. "See you later," she said colorlessly.

Shit, I thought, as Katie Bell walked away. I felt a bitter twinge of regret and anger at myself. Why had I been so embarrassed of my best friend? All she'd wanted was a picture.

For the first time, I felt the ground below Katie Bell and I cracking. I watched her, hoping she might turn, but she didn't. She rejoined Molly and Amanda, who were not exactly dancing but were now at least moving their hips to the beat of the music.

My blooming guilt, however, was swiftly overshadowed as I realized Ransome and Buzz were walking up to the bleachers. They both sat, splay-legged, on the bench below ours.

"Hey," said Ransome. It was to all of us, but the way he tilted his head just slightly in my direction made me feel like the greeting was intended especially for me. My stomach flipped as I offered a weak "hey" back.

From where I was sitting behind him, I could see the curve of Ransome's jaw and the long slope of his nose. The back of his neck was tanned a deep reddish brown from hours on the boat, and his hair curled just slightly at the nape of his neck, where it came to a V. That detail, like something private between us, made me smile.

None of us said anything for a while as we watched the campers finally mix. It was different from when we were out at the riflery range. The banter that came so easily on those nights escaped us here. Somehow what we talked about at the riflery range didn't seem appropriate at the dance, surrounded by campers, Fred and Marjorie, and Abe. It would have seemed too sarcastic and out of place.

Before long, there was only a sliver of sun peeking over the low mountains. Someone threw the switch on the floodlights at the four corners of the tennis court. They flickered for a moment, buzzing and popping, and then bathed us all in a bluish-white glow. The few couples dancing paused, and then resumed rocking back and forth.

"Whoa!" exclaimed Winn, blinking at the sudden brightness, and we all laughed a little harder than we needed to.

I saw Ruby spot me from across the court, where she was jumping up and down like a pogo stick with Melanie and Abby. Her mouth drew into an excited O. She grabbed Melanie's hand and proceeded to drag her across the court toward us, nearly tripping over her own feet and the few campers who had actually coupled in the middle of the lonely dance floor. The two girls bumped to a stop in front of the bleachers.

"Helena," Ruby fretted, "why aren't you dancing?"

Winn and the other girls laughed at Ruby's undeniable cuteness. Even on Ransome's face I thought I detected the beginnings of a smile.

"I'm having fun watching you dance!" I assured her.

Ruby gave me an impatient look and set her fists on her tiny hips. Then she pouted, sticking her lower lip out comically. It was something she knew worked on almost every counselor at camp, including me.

"Well," I said, giving in, "I don't have anyone to dance with. Would you dance with me?"

"No," Ruby announced. She lunged at Ransome, grabbing his hands. "You're gonna dance with *him*!"

My eyes widened to take in Ransome's reaction. He was grinning at Ruby, apparently ready to humor her.

"Are you sure you wanna see me dance?" he asked her. "I'll warn you. It's not a pretty sight."

I ha-ha'ed nervously.

"It's true," Winn teased. She shot him with a tiny squirt of her Super Soaker.

"Hey!" he exclaimed at the wet spot on his shirt. Winn laughed.

"Yes. I want to see." Ruby tossed her head up and down in an emphatic nod, and Ransome pretended to let her pull his weight from the bench.

"Well," he said, offering me his hand, "shall we?"

"I guess so," I answered, trying to maintain some semblance of composure while actually undergoing a full internal freak-out.

Ruby and Melanie jumped up and down, clapping their hands. Melanie grabbed my elbow and Ruby grabbed Ransome's, and they pulled us behind them onto the dance floor, where Dr. Spin was playing a song by ABBA. I was relieved for a fast song, unsure of how we'd dance to a slow one. Ransome spun Ruby in a circle, then me, alternating between us until we were dizzy. But after a couple quick choruses of

"Dancing Queen," the song ended. And sure enough, the low, plodding beat of a slow song took over.

Giggling, Ruby and Melanie locked their hands around each other's necks and swayed back and forth in imitation of the more sincere couples around them. Unsure whether I was supposed to retreat back to the bleachers with the other counselors now, I reluctantly raised my eyes to Ransome's.

Without hesitation, he took my right hand in his and rested the other on my back, and we proceeded to rock back and forth from foot to foot. He was right; he wasn't a good dancer, and we were a consistent millisecond off-beat as we stepped in a tight, jerky circle. But he smelled good, like a mixture of Pert Plus and Old Spice and that *guy* smell that lingered on you and that you never wanted to go away, so much so that you'd avoid washing your clothes as long as possible within the realm of acceptability.

Our bodies were a safe distance from touching, but his hand was warm through my tissue-thin shirt, its weight tentative on the small of my back. I was aware that his face, only a few inches from mine, was tilted down, as if he might whisper something in my ear any second. Insanely nervous, I kept my eyes from meeting his by looking everywhere but into his face. I was scared he'd read all the thoughts zipping through my head and even suspect I'd put Ruby up to this.

Finally, I had to speak.

"Are you going to the riflery range tonight?" I tried to sound casual.

"No," he said, and I hoped the letdown I heard in his voice came from the same place my disappointment did. "I'm COD."

"That sucks. I was just COD." As soon as I said it I wanted to swallow the words. It was a stupid throw-away comment—every counselor was on duty at some point. Why couldn't I think of something real to say to him?

Ransome didn't seem to notice. He explained that he was covering for another counselor who wanted the night off to be with his girlfriend; she'd driven two hours to see him. I hardly caught the details, though, because I was focused on the fact that, in the process of talking, Ransome had pulled me—just slightly—closer to him, so that I felt his body brush against mine. It was suddenly hard for me to breathe. Aside from being tall, Ransome wasn't a big guy, but I was fascinated by how his muscles moved like cables under his skin. His body had a solidness that made me very aware I was dancing with a man, not a boy. My heart was battering so loudly against my chest that I wondered if this wasn't the beat Ransome's feet were following instead of the music.

As the final notes of the song drifted from Dr. Spin's speakers, Ransome lifted my hand above my head and spun me once before dipping me so close to the ground I was afraid he was going to drop me on the green concrete. He didn't, and managed to raise me back up to standing with a wide grin on his face.

"Thanks for the dance," he said, his arm still around my waist.

"Thank *you*," I said coyly. "You're only twice as bad as you say." He laughed.

It seemed like Ransome released my hand teasingly, one finger at a time, not fully letting it slip from his until we'd turned toward the bleachers, where more counselors had gathered.

I'm sure we walked back to them the normal way, with one foot rising and moving forward to meet the earth, and then the other, but in my mind I was floating two inches above the ground.

Chapter 8

My drugstore flip-flops slapped at my heels as I shuffled to the Bath with a beach towel on my arm. The bugle would call for dinner soon, but it didn't matter. I had the night off.

An earthy aroma of mildew, covered by the sharp smell of Clorox, wafted from the showers. One shower-head was running, and a cloud of steam rose from behind the curtain. I was surprised when the water stopped and out stepped Katie Bell with a pink towel piled on top of her head and another wrapped under her arms. A bath pouf dangled from her wrist.

I'd barely seen Katie Bell since the dance on Saturday, and it was already Tuesday. Table seating in the Mess changed every week, so Katie Bell had moved to Table Two, and the Sharks hadn't been scheduled for swimming yet that week. I was feeling guilty again for the way I'd acted about the photo with her at the dance. Twice I'd been to her cabin looking for her, hoping things would be normal again. But her cabinmates had said she was gone—maybe with Molly and Amanda, or at the barn? They didn't know, they shrugged. Had I checked the waterfront? Maybe she was trying out one of the new Sunfish sailboats Fred had just bought. But there had been no wind that day. I had the sneaking suspicion that Katie Bell was avoiding me.

She jumped, startled, when she saw me. The showers were usually empty by this time.

I laughed. "Hey."

"Hey," she answered, quickly reassembling her cool attitude.

"Where have you been?"

Katie Bell avoided my gaze, looking instead at the lockers behind me, her shower shoes, anywhere but my face.

"I don't know." She shrugged, which dislodged her towel. She quickly retucked it. "Around."

Something had clearly slipped off the tracks between us, but I didn't know how to fix it. Apologizing wasn't the answer I was looking for. I hadn't *done* anything. It was just how I'd felt, what I'd thought. How could you apologize for that? Better to just make up for

116

it, I figured. Say something . . .

"I feel like it's been a while," I tried.

Katie Bell's hip jutted beneath her towel. "Yeah," she agreed. To anyone else her tone might have sounded bored, maybe tired, but I knew that tone and I knew Katie Bell. I knew that that tone meant Katie Bell was pissed.

Still, I tried to smooth things over. "Can we hang out soon? I'll bring the Pixy Stix," I added.

Katie Bell's expression softened a nanometer. A few years earlier we'd discovered we could bribe younger campers to turn over the Pixy Stix they received in their care packages. One summer we'd convinced our entire cabin to write home specifically requesting the colorful paper tubes filled with flavored sugar. When they arrived, we greedily ripped them open and dumped the sugar down our throats. We'd even sniffed it up our noses. That had been Katie Bell's idea. It had made our eyes water and noses sting and caused a nasty crash an hour later, but the sugar high was unparalleled.

"Like we used to," I pressed on.

Katie Bell's face hardened again, the parentheses that had formed from the corners of her nose to her chin disappearing.

"Well," she said, turning to put her bath caddy, filled with shampoo, soap, and razor, back on top of the lockers, "it's not like it used to be, is it?"

Her comment stung, partly for the truth of it.

"Come on, Katie Bell," I urged. "Don't be like that."

"Like what?" she said fiercely, turning to face me again with her gunmetal eyes.

"Like that." I smiled, hoping she would too. "I miss hanging out with you."

"Fine," she said, rolling her head and eyes dramatically. "I miss you too. Come to my cabin after dinner. And come bearing Pixy Stix."

As I started to agree I suddenly remembered about my night off.

"Shoot!" My stomach dropped. "I can't tonight. It's my night off. I'm just showering before we leave. I'm going with Winn and some people to the pizza place in town. . . . Can we do it tomorrow?" I asked hopefully.

"Whatever," said Katie Bell, moving around me for the door. Whatever, as in, No. Whatever, as in, I knew you didn't mean it. Whatever, as in, You're a bitch.

Before I could respond, Katie Bell had stepped out into the sideways sunlight and was stalking up the path to the cabins.

"Katie Bell," I started to call after her, but the words stuck in my throat like a pill that was too big to swallow.

Later, as I lathered my hair under the water that was

starting to go cold, I grew increasingly annoyed until I was finally angry. Katie Bell was right; I knew that. I'd known it since the night of the dance and probably even before that: things weren't like they used to be. But it wasn't my fault! It wasn't my fault that I had been born three months before Katie Bell or that somehow in the past year I had managed to grow up when she hadn't.

I realized my fingernails were digging into my scalp as I scrubbed. Under the lukewarm shower, I closed my eyes and let the suds run down my back and face. I wiped the soap from my scrunched eyes, really trying to wipe away my frustration with Katie Bell.

"Whatever," I repeated out loud, echoing her words. I didn't have time to dwell on it. I had to get dressed to meet Winn and the others at the Mansion. We were going to Mama Mia's, the ancient pizza place off the highway to town, and then bowling. A few Brownies were meeting us, Ransome included, and while no one in her right mind would construe this night as a date, I had the first-date jitters. Pull it together, Hel, I thought. It's game time.

The dark shapes of trees zoomed by in the night. Unbelievably, I found myself sitting on Ransome's lap in the back of Buzz's car. Sarah had gone back to camp early because of explosive digestive issues she'd told the boys was a headache, leaving us all to ride back with Buzz. When Lizbeth, Winn, Ransome, and I had wedged into the backseat, Ransome had suggested I just sit on his lap. I deflated when Winn offered to sit in the way back, but Saint Buzz pointed out it was full of skeet-shooting stuff. I'd quickly, and gratefully, climbed onto Ransome's lap before any other arrangements could be made.

I was slightly drunk. At the Strike 'n' Spare, the Brownies had bought pitchers of flat beer with their fake IDs, and the one slice of greasy pizza I'd barely eaten at Mama Mia's was not doing its supposed job of soaking up the alcohol. My feet were tingly and my head felt warm and fuzzy. And although my energy was focused on seeming light and petite in Ransome's lap—by shoving my foot under the seat in front of me and propping my weight uncomfortably on one side—I kept returning to the thought of Fred and Marjorie smelling the alcohol on our breath when we checked in back at camp.

I glanced at the glowing numbers on the dashboard of Buzz's SUV—a typical guy car: papers and wrappers littered the floor, boxes of skeet clays slid around the trunk every time we turned, and several empty cans of dip had infused the car with a stale, sweet, tobacco smell. The clock informed me it was only nine forty-five.

"We have an hour," Winn said, reading my mind. "What do y'all want to do?"

"There's that overlook at the end of the old logging road," Ben offered from the passenger seat. The poor guy probably had no idea he'd reinforced his reputation with Winn and Sarah as a dud by being mostly silent the whole night. This was the first thing he'd said in hours.

Winn and Lizbeth looked at each other, considering the idea.

"Let's go," Winn decided. As she said it, she tossed her blond hair over her shoulder in this way that let you know she was a girl up for anything. She, for one, didn't seem to be worrying about a sobriety test from our camp parents at the end of the evening. That was apparently left to nervous JCs like myself.

"Yeah," Ransome agreed enthusiastically. "Let's go there."

Behind me, his mouth was so close to my ear, I could feel his breath. Barely, imperceptibly, I let my weight settle into his lap. Ransome gave Buzz directions to the access for the logging road. And as he did, he felt for my hand in the dark. My heart did a somersault into my throat.

Ransome's fingers were long and cool. They were rough from tying and untying a million times the ropes that secured the motorboats. He wrapped them over my hand, which curled in his palm, and hooked his thumb around mine. A warm rush swept from the center of my body down to my toes and to the top of my head.

"Hang a right, here," he instructed, and Buzz swung his headlights in a sharp arc onto the dark, overgrown road.

The music on the radio (country, but I was too pre-occupied at the moment to hate it), punctuated by Winn and Lizbeth's delighted shrieks as we were jostled over the bumpy road, filled the car. But in my head, there was a stunned, expectant silence. This was the first time Ransome and I had really touched—not accidental or in-cidental, but like he meant it. He *wanted* to touch me.

Buzz's headlights illuminated tangled branches and bushes that choked the side of the road. Just as I started to worry maybe we were getting ourselves lost, the woods thinned and we came to a rocky clearing where the road seemed to drop abruptly over a cliff. Below, the lake spread out in front of us. I'd never seen it from this height.

Buzz threw the car into park and killed the engine, leaving the lights on to shine over the abyss.

"Do you think we need to turn those off?" I asked. I had an irrational fear that Fred would see the headlights from a window of the Mansion and know immediately that it was us. Not that we were doing anything wrong. At least not yet.

Ransome shook his head. "Nah."

The sound of car doors slamming echoed across the lake, slapping against the water and exposed rock. The others drifted toward the edge of the cliff, where Buzz was already standing, peeing over the side, and I started to follow. Ransome, still holding my hand, gently pulled me back.

"Do you want to sit here?" he asked, motioning with his head to the car. "It's more comfortable."

I nodded. He released my hand and lifted his weight up and back onto the hood in one swift, smooth motion. I tried to do the same, but my mouth puckered into a surprised "Oh!" when I heard the small tinny thump of metal denting.

Ransome laughed. "Don't worry. This bucket has taken a lot worse. Buzz was shooting at it with a pellet gun the other day."

As my nervous laugh hung in the air, we both studied the view. The lake reflected the moonlight like ribbons of mercury. The shore was fringed with docks, and through the treetops, I could make out the roofs of some of the cabins and historic cottages that made this lake a favorite vacation spot for generations of families.

At the far point of the lake, where it hooked slightly to the right and narrowed, I thought I could see Southpoint's floating dock and, beyond that, a small clearing dotted by tiny buildings.

"Oh my gosh!" I pointed. "Is that camp? Are those the cabins?" I thought of my campers tucked snugly (I hoped) into their bunks.

Ransome leaned across me to see where my finger was pointing. Our heads almost touched, and his bare arm, below the sleeve of his T-shirt, brushed against mine. It was warm that night, and I hadn't had to wear the pullover now lying in the backseat of Buzz's car.

"Yep," Ransome said, a little less awed than I was to see camp so distant and small. I guessed he'd seen this view before, having grown up here.

"That's so cool," I whispered. It looked like a tiny doll village.

I leaned forward and narrowed my eyes to better make out the individual cabins, picking out mine, but Ransome didn't move back to his side of the hood. Our legs were now touching from hip to knee.

"So where do you come from, Helena?"

The random question surprised me, so I laughed.

"Nashville," I answered uneasily. Ransome knew where I was from. He'd asked the first night out at the riflery range.

"I know." He grinned irresistibly. "I guess I mean more like . . . what's your story?"

I examined his face for sincerity and smiled when I

found it waiting there for me. "You want my life story?" I teased.

"Sure." He reclined back on the hood of the car, interlacing his fingers behind his head. "Lay it on me." He smiled. "But keep in mind we only have an hour."

I lay down next to him. The night was clear except for a few wispy clouds that skittered over the moon. "Well, it all started in a small delivery room at Vanderbilt Hospital. . . ." I began.

He poked me in the ribs, which tickled, and I squirmed.

"I'm kidding," I said, settling down to actually think about the question. No one, especially no guy, had ever asked me something on the surface so casual, but quietly deep.

I had always thought Ransome was worthy of my crush. He was older and mysterious and cute. But now, suddenly, he seemed worthy of more, worthy of opening up for, worthy of trusting. Ransome the fantasy was slowly becoming Ransome the real person, and a real person I desperately wanted to kiss in real life.

I wished I had a better answer for him. "I don't know how I became who I am," I observed honestly. "I mean, I grew up pretty normal. Ballet lessons, piano lessons, swimming lessons . . ."

I paused, remembering back to the times I'd

been happy—and the times I hadn't. Things had been great right before my father left, everyone getting along and smiling at each other, saying "please" and "thank you" at the dinner table. We even went to the beach that summer, right before it all fell apart. The calm before the storm. Then he was gone and the cloud descended, the one that had kept my mom in bed for days at a time and made me wish I could live at camp.

"Then my parents got divorced," I said, "and things haven't been so normal since, I guess. Or whatever's considered normal."

Ransome was quiet. I waited for him to say something to chase away the seriousness that had crept into our conversation. But he didn't.

I bit my lip. It tasted like the cherry Chap Stick I always kept in my pocket. "He left us—my dad," I explained. "A few years ago, for another woman."

At this revelation I stopped, not because I was afraid of what Ransome would say, but because I was afraid of what *I* would. Despite a year of weekly therapy sessions, in which my mother's shrink made me draw stupid pictures (like I was a four-year-old who couldn't use her words) and talk about my birth (like I could remember), this was still the point of the story where my voice became bitter and strange, even to myself. I didn't want to cry in front of Ransome.

"Jeez. That's hard," he said, exhaling. "You know my parents are divorced," he added.

I did know. Everyone at Southpoint knew Abe. And while there was no one left who remembered Ransome's mother, we all knew that Abe was divorced and had essentially raised Ransome on his own.

"It's not easy, ya know?" Not far away, the others were talking loudly, oblivious to the conversation going on on the hood of the car. Still, Ransome lowered his voice. "I kind of know how you feel. Everyone thinks the reason my mom left my dad was because he was in love with Marjorie."

It turned my heart cold to think of Fred and Marjorie and Abe caught in a love triangle. They were different. They were camp parents. They were supposed to live by a higher code.

Ransome turned his head to look at me, maybe to see if I had heard the rumor too. I hadn't. "That wasn't the reason?" I asked.

"No," he said, almost defensively. "They were just always fighting about money. . . . But just knowing people thought that, that they were *saying* it . . . People forget they're not just camp directors or bosses, ya know? They're my family, *my real* family."

I nodded slowly, chewing on the inside of my cheek. Ransome's voice was steady, no signs of cracking, like mine did when I talked about these things.

"I can imagine," I said.

Ransome was quietly staring up at the sky.

"Are they looking?" he asked.

"Who?"

"The others. Winn and Buzz and them."

I lifted my head to see that Buzz had everyone's full attention. He was telling a story and gesturing wildly with his hands, which had Winn and Lizbeth clutching at each other in spasms of laughter.

"Nope," I said, lying back down. "They're not looking."

"Good," said Ransome, and then his mouth was on mine.

Completely startled, I met him with stiff lips and clenched teeth. It took my brain a second to register what was happening. Then, realizing that Ransome was actually kissing me, my mouth gave way, opening to his.

The inside of his mouth was warm and tasted like beer and mint. As I moved my head, he lowered the weight of his upper body across my chest. One of his hands was tangled in my hair. My body reacted to his movements instinctively, but my mind was going haywire. Was this seriously happening? Could I really be kissing the one guy in the world I had spent *years* of my life fantasizing about? That didn't happen in the real world. It happened in movies and romance novels.

Holy crap. I was making out with Ransome.

Our weight must have shifted, because suddenly the hood beneath us thumped. We sprang apart and peeked at the ledge to see if the others had noticed. For a split second, Winn inclined her face in our direction. I was sure she'd seen us, but she quickly turned back to Buzz.

Flustered, I lightly pushed Ransome away and sat up straight, pulling my hair from its mussed ponytail and tying it back up. He sat up too, and we looked at each other, speechless for a moment. . . . Busted. A smile cracked on both of our faces, and he chuckled.

"Maybe we should get them," he said, the smile still crinkling the corners of his eyes as he nodded toward the others. "It's getting close to eleven, and we have to take y'all home before we get back to camp."

Ransome offered me his hand as I pushed myself off the car. Again the hood made the pop-pop-thump sound, and we both laughed, although I could have done without the auditory reminder that I was not a waif.

Before he released my hand, Ransome gave it a tiny squeeze. He jogged to say something to the others about the time, but I lagged behind, tugging at the bottom of my shirt and trying unsuccessfully to slow my racing heartbeat. Turning so that no one could see me, I mouthed "Thank you" silently to the woods.

* * *

"Um, y'all . . ." I said shakily once we were out of Buzz's car and walking up the gravel road to the Mansion. Despite the fact that Buzz had had to gun it on the curvy country roads to get us there before curfew, we'd arrived back at camp on time and in one piece.

Part of me knew I should wait to tell Katie Bell first, but I couldn't hold it in. The effort might have killed me. "Ransome kissed me," I said.

"He did? Really?" The surprise in Winn's reply struck me as odd. I thought she'd caught us up at the point.

But Lizbeth burst, "I knew it!" as if there'd been some speculation.

My head was swimming. "We were talking, and he just kind of . . . laid one on me."

"Wow," Winn replied slowly. "That doesn't sound like Ransome. He must really like you."

"I don't know," I said. I was still in shock. "I hope so." Understatement.

We'd reached the back stairs to the Mansion by that point, where the porch light was on for us. My stomach worked itself into a new set of knots as we tiptoed into the house. I was terrified Fred would smell the beer on our breath. I couldn't bring myself even to imagine disappointing Fred and Marjorie. It'd be like dropkicking Mother Teresa. So when we stuck our heads in the office door to let Fred know we were home, I stayed toward the back and let Winn do the talking. All clear. She was a pro.

"Good night, girls," Fred called after us, switching out the lights in the office. "Get some sleep."

Winn, Lizbeth, and I looked at each other with wide eyes and giggled as we quickly shuffled out of the house, wondering how much more Fred knew than we thought he did.

I could have stayed up talking about Ransome all night, but at the Bath, Winn and Lizbeth whispered "Good night" and headed for their beds. I retreated to my cabin, where privately (or semi-privately, in a cabin full of eight- and nine-year-olds) I could replay my kiss with Ransome until I drifted off into a deliriously happy sleep.

Chapter 9

The first thing my tired eyes saw the next morning was Ruby's upside-down cherubic face inches from mine. Standing at the head of my bed, she was studying my face intently, perhaps to check that I was still breathing.

"Wake up, sleepyhead!" she cried with that tiny hint of a lisp that was usually adorable, but was, at the moment, incredibly annoying.

I groaned and shut my eyes again. "Ruby," I said hoarsely, "what time is it? Shhh. Get back in your bunk until Reveille."

She giggled. "Reveille already blew, silly. You missed Flag Raising!"

I shot up in my bed, fully awake now. "What? What time is it? Really, the bugle already blew?"

"Yes," Ruby said impatiently.

Sure enough, all around me, my campers were already straightening their shoes under their beds and stepping into the cleanest shorts left in their trunks.

"Are you sick?" Melanie, who also stood by my bed now, asked suspiciously. Since the spider eggs in the chin incident, she and Ruby had been inseparable. Kind of like Katie Bell and I had been once upon a time.

"No," I said, swinging my creaky body around to stand. From the beer at the bowling alley, my brain felt a couple sizes too big for my head. It didn't matter, though. Once my initial alarm at having slept through Flag Raising subsided, the memory of the previous night's kiss seeped through my body like warm water. Brief as it had been, it was the best kiss of my life.

I wanted to kick my legs, grab Ruby in a bear hug, sweep Melanie into a waltz around the cabin, and tell the girls they could have the day off of inspection, because their counselor had officially kissed the love of her life last night. I also thought of running to tell Katie Bell, but the way we had left each other at the Bath the day before stopped me. Instead I sat on the edge of my bed and let the dizziness fade as the girls cleaned up and dressed for breakfast.

Finally, I raised myself from the warmth of the bed and went to my trunk to find something to wear. As I reached for a bathing suit, I remembered it was Field Day.

The campers didn't know yet because it hadn't been announced, but that day was one of the biggest at camp. At breakfast they'd be divided into the East and West Teams, according to which side of the cabin they lived on. The teams would compete in a day of relay races and field games, ending in a swim meet and, just before sundown, a mini-marathon. The team that accumulated the most points throughout the day was pronounced the winner. At ceremonies on closing day, that team would select one girl, usually a cubby, who had most embodied the Southpoint spirit at Field Day. She received the Spirit Award, and her name was stenciled in either green or white (Easts were green, Wests were white) by the crafts counselor on a plaque that hung over the Mess door for future generations to admire and revere. Last year it was Pookie. The year before it had been Winn.

I fished out the one-piece I normally wore on Field Day, an old swim team bathing suit cut for speed rather than style, then quickly reconsidered at the thought of Ransome swinging by the swim meet on a ski boat. I pictured him waving from behind the wheel, and instead shimmied into a black bikini.

After breakfast, while the campers were at a special Morning Gathering, where Marjorie stressed the importance of teamwork, perseverance, and a positive attitude, the counselors were busy setting up games and outfitting for the day. Every Field Day had a theme, and the counselors costumed accordingly. The previous year's had been the Olympics, in celebration of the summer games going on in some faraway country. The counselors had wrapped themselves in togas made from bedsheets and towels. This year it had been declared by Nan, the oldest counselor, who'd been at Southpoint for as long as I could remember, and Winn, that we would be Gladiators—of the red, white, and blue spandex–wearing American variety. Thanks to Hulk Hogan and a brilliant television executive, *American Gladiators* had made a comeback that summer. Because, really, what could be more fun than mixing steroids, baby oil, and padded helmets?

We had scoured our trunks and the camp costume bags, which were stuffed with moldy polyester costumes and Salvation Army finds. And when we reconvened at Cabin Five before trekking together to Death Valley, each counselor who walked up in sweatbands or a unitard drew a new wave of laughter. I cracked up when Lila approached, grinning, in nothing but a turquoise blue leotard, white kneesocks scrunched over her ankles, and tennis shoes. When Pookie came up in a sports bra emblazoned with the Gladiator name STEALTH, and a permanent marker tattoo that said

I ♥ JOUSTING, it was all over. We looked back and forth at each other and doubled over, laughing so hard we were dangerously close to peeing our spandex pants.

Still slightly delirious from the night before, everything seemed funny to me—or almost everything. There were two things bothering me. One, I still hadn't smoothed things over with Katie Bell. And two, I'd been trying to shove to the back of my mind since breakfast, but it wouldn't stay put: maybe I was crazy, but I couldn't shake the feeling that Winn was ignoring me.

She hadn't come by my table at breakfast like she normally did, and when I looked over at her now to share a laugh over our ridiculous outfits, it was like she wasn't seeing me *on purpose*. She was focusing a little *too* intently on the person in front of her, turning her back to me, or angling her face so that I was just out of sight, so that she *couldn't* see the hilariously huge silver belt I'd cinched around my waist (the black bikini set aside for later), or the boxing gloves and knee pads I'd dug out from the back of the sporting equipment locker. When I did catch Winn's eyes, once, she turned quickly, her blond ponytail flashing. Even the overly loud laughter she was sharing with Sarah, Lizbeth, Caroline, Lila, Pookie, Marge—anyone and everyone but me—felt forced and punishing, a sure sign that she was mad at me.

Quickly, the fun I was having dressing up for my first Field Day as a counselor was slipping away and being replaced by a heavy nauseating feeling in the pit of my stomach.

Nan and Winn conferred on the cabin porch over a piece of paper. "Okay," Winn finally shouted.

Nan put two fingers in her mouth and whistled above our talking. "Are we all here?" She did a quick head count.

"When the bugle blows," Winn said, still avoiding my gaze, "we'll all run down to meet the campers. Except for me and Sarah. We'll come back to the dock to get ready for the lake events." She looked at Sarah and nodded.

I frowned, confused. I was a swim counselor too. Without thinking, I raised my hand. "Winn, do you need me to help at the dock?"

Her eyes met mine for the first time that day. "No, we got it, Helena," she said. "Just go down with the counselors, and they'll show you what to do."

Puzzled, I glanced around to see if anyone else had heard the condescension in her voice, but the bugle blew. The counselors gathered their lances and shields, improvised from brooms, hockey sticks, pool noodles, and trash can lids, and headed down the path toward Death Valley.

Winn ducked into her cabin, so I hung back, waiting for her to come out again. When she did, I caught her by the elbow. "Winn, is everything okay?"

She slid her sunglasses from her head down over her eyes. "Of course," she said quickly. "Everything's fine. Why wouldn't it be?"

I wasn't sure, and was opening my mouth to say so when she said, "I'll see you down at Death Valley," and turned to shout something to Nan about the tug-of-war rope. I had been dismissed.

"Chew! Chew! Chew!" the girls chanted from both sides of the sideline.

As they screamed at the top of their lungs, Rachel, a tall knock-kneed girl from Six East, stood in front of me spewing chunks of saltine crackers. If she could swallow the crackers, manage a whistle, and tag Katie Bell, the last person in her team's relay line, before her opponent, the Easts might win this event and pull ahead. So she focused and puckered.

I bent closer to Rachel's mouth and heard a sharp whistle. Nodding, I tapped her on the shoulder, and she wheeled toward Katie Bell. Rachel slapped her hand, and Katie Bell was off. As she skidded to a stop in front of me, I smiled, but Katie Bell didn't smile back. Her face was a freckled mask of concentration as she lunged for the last two crackers on the plate I held out. Cramming them into her mouth, she chewed with determination. Her eyebrows strained toward each other, crinkling the skin at the bridge of her nose. All of Katie Bell's energy was focused on winning this event. Finally she managed to swallow the gummy mass and pull her lips into a circle, but when she blew, all that came out was the sound of rushing air. I bent closer to listen for even the vaguest notion of a whistle. Nothing.

She was flapping her hands now in frustration. Still no sound but the tacky smack of her tongue against the roof of her mouth as she swallowed and tried again. Her frantic eyes met mine for a half second, and as they did, before I registered what I was doing, I tapped her on the shoulder.

The look that flickered across Katie Bell's face was a combination of surprise, disapproval, and gratitude. I nodded to clear her for takeoff, and as I did, a thin whistle escaped her lips.

Katie Bell arrived at the finish line two steps ahead of her challenger, where she flopped victorious and out of breath on the ground. Her team went wild, jumping up and down. A beaming Katie Bell got to her feet and went to join them.

As a counselor I was supposed to be neutral, but *I* wanted to jump up and down and hug Katie Bell and cheer until my head hurt from screaming so loud too.

I also wanted to pull Katie Bell aside and tell her that I'd kissed Ransome last night. Whatever frustrations had surfaced between us yesterday outside the showers, I wanted them to be gone. I needed to tell my best friend about this. Still, it wasn't until after the egg toss, while the counselors were adding last-minute buckets of water to the mud pit beneath the tug-of-war rope, that I had a second to steal Katie Bell away from her teammates.

"Hey," I whispered excitedly as I quietly pulled her aside.

"Hey," she replied. "Why are we whispering?"

I laughed, not realizing I had been. "Sorry. I just want to tell you something."

Katie Bell perked up. Even if she was still harboring irritation from yesterday, she would always be a sucker for a secret. Glancing around, I pulled her farther away from the other campers and counselors gathering for the tug-of-war.

"Ransome kissed me last night."

"Really?"

I nodded, laughing. "Can you believe it? I'm so . . . freaked out! I mean, *I made out with Ransome*."

"That's awesome, Hel," said Katie Bell. But she was a

bit more underwhelmed than I'd expected. What was with everyone? Could *someone* be giddy with me, please?

"Are you excited?" Her question was clunky and wooden, and the obviousness of the answer annoyed me.

"Well, yeah!" I said. Of course I was excited, although the smile had started to wilt on my face. "We drove out to this point that overlooks the whole lake, and we were talking on the hood of Buzz's car, and—"

Distracted, Katie Bell glanced over at the tug-of-war pit. The rest of the cubbies were starting to line up on either end, and Winn was walking up to retrieve Katie Bell for the Easts.

"Shhh," Katie Bell said quickly. "Here comes Winn."

"It's okay. She knows."

Katie Bell's eyes flashed to my face. "You already told her?"

"Yeah," I said, wishing I hadn't told Katie Bell that. I started to explain that Winn was there when it happened, but she was right in front of us.

"Katie Bell, we're ready to start. You coming?"

"Yeah," said Katie Bell quickly. Then to me, "We can talk about this later, right?"

"Yeah. Of course," I assured her, reminding myself that we were in the middle of Field Day. "Have fun. Get muddy. Just don't even *think* about dragging me in."

Every year, a few counselors, usually the cubbies'

favorites, got dragged into the mud after them. The mud pit was a fun, if disgusting, experience that required a shower before being allowed into the Mess for lunch.

"Don't worry," Katie Bell said in a tone that wasn't mean, just . . . indifferent. "I won't pull you in."

She jogged to take her place at the front of the rope and, when the whistle blew, dug her heels into the ground. The Wests made short business of the Easts, and Katie Bell was true to her word. She didn't pull me into the mud, but as I watched the other counselors get dragged into the chocolate-brown slop, I knew I had kind of wanted her to.

It took *forever* for the other counselors to leave the riflery range that night. When I'd gotten there, Ransome had looked straight at me, and a nervousness that had been weighing on me since that afternoon lifted.

Ransome hadn't come by the swim meet that day like I'd imagined. Because of that, I'd worked myself into a state of panic and paranoia that maybe he hadn't meant to kiss me the night before at all. Maybe it had been a freak accident. He'd fallen onto my face, and I'd assaulted him by sticking my tongue down his throat. Or worse, maybe it was a bet. Or a prank.

We'd just been talking about our own prank on our way to the range—the mattress-on-the-floating-dock idea

I'd had the first night. Winn was a COD, thankfully, but Pookie and I had gone with Sarah, Lizbeth, and Caroline out there after Taps. They were debating whether to pull our prank now, or whether the guys would be expecting that and we should wait another week to heighten the suspense. So it felt entirely possible that Buzz and Nate and the other Brownies had put Ransome up to kissing me at the overlook as part of the prank war. They could have orchestrated the whole night just to make a poor little JC think a Brownie demigod actually liked her. Sick, sick people.

But when I'd ducked into the riflery hut, Ransome hadn't looked away or down or pointed and laughed (worst case scenario but certainly not out of the realm of my neurotic imagination). He'd looked straight at me and smiled like we had a secret, and I'd melted.

Like the first night at the range, he'd scooted over on the mattress so I could sit next to him. Only it wasn't as crowded this time as it had been that first night, and unfortunately there was no reason for me to sit nearly on top of him. It was killing me sitting so close without touching him. Just pinky-to-pinky would have been enough.

Instead I had to focus on a conversation about Nate's genetic inability to curl his tongue like normal people could. The latter part of that statement was currently being debated, as Pookie and Caroline's sister evidently couldn't do it either.

"What I'm *saying*," said Nate, "is that the vast majority of the population can fold their tongue."

"Do you *know* it's a majority?" asked Lizbeth. "Maybe we're not a good sample."

It wasn't scintillating conversation. At any moment, I waited for Ransome to stand and stretch and say he was calling it a night. Every twitch of his arm and repositioning of his legs caused a little flutter of panic in me that he was leaving. As long as Ransome stayed, I'd stay. It was the waiting game. But it wasn't until everyone but Buzz, Sarah, Ransome, and I were left that I realized we were *both* playing the waiting game.

Ransome spit into his Gatorade bottle and tapped at the round tin of dip he'd pulled from his back pocket. Now that there were only four of us, it was quiet at the range. The only sounds were the crickets and frogs at the lake.

"I don't know how y'all stand that stuff," said Sarah, nodding at Ransome's dip.

Buzz packed a fat wad in his bottom lip. "You wanna try it?"

"No." Sarah made a face. "You tried that last year, remember, and I almost threw up."

"Helena?" Buzz offered his tin in my direction.

"Thanks, I'll pass," I said. Maybe a guy could pull

it off, but I couldn't imagine that a girl dipping would be very attractive. I pictured a dribble of brown drool dripping off my chin.

"Did y'all hear what our cubbies did?" asked Ransome, changing the subject.

Sarah and I both shook our heads.

"Somehow they snuck into the office to copy photos of Beverly and then posted them on the targets at the archery range."

"What?!" Sarah was cracking up. "Shut up. No they didn't. Abe would kill them."

Beverly was the camp nurse for both Brownstone and Southpoint, who obviously hated what she did, because there was not a single time in my nine years there that I had seen her smile. Campers would go a week with a stomachache before they'd go see Beverly. Once when a horse stepped on Katie Bell's foot at the barn, she'd limped around for days before Marjorie noticed and made her go see a foot doctor in town.

"No, it's true!" said Buzz. "We haven't told Abe yet."

"I don't believe you," said Sarah, raising a leery eyebrow. I could tell she was wondering if this was some part of an elaborate prank.

"Come see 'em, then," said Buzz. He stood and obviously expected Sarah to as well. "We haven't taken them down yet. We're gonna give 'em a couple more days. I have to say, I was kind of proud of the guys."

I laughed. "Y'all are evil."

Sure, Beverly was mean, but maybe she was just lonely. (As far as we knew, there was no Mr. Beverly.) There had to be something that kept her coming back to camp. She definitely didn't deserve to be target practice.

Ransome acknowledged this. "I know. We really should take them down, Buzz. Someone's gonna slip up and tell Dad."

"Come on," said Buzz. He extended a hand to pull Sarah from the floor. "I want to show you if you won't believe me."

Now I saw where this was going. Winn had been right. Buzz wanted to go somewhere so they could hook up. Smooth, I thought, amazed at Buzz's unexpected tact.

"Fine." Sarah acted like she was giving in as she stood up, but I could tell from the hint of embarrassment in her voice that she knew exactly what Buzz was trying to do, and probably knew from the beginning that she would go with him.

I kind of wanted to chuckle. It was fun watching someone else squirm when I felt just as anxious about being left alone with Ransome.

We watched Buzz and Sarah walk off in the dark

toward the archery range. I wondered if this was the first time they'd hooked up this summer, or if Sarah had managed to keep it from us. I was sure Winn would be giving her hell if she knew.

"So," said Ransome. He had moved to the mattress across from me so that we were facing each other now. He sat with his elbows crooked over his knees.

"So," I said, smiling and trying not to fill the awkward silence with a laugh. It would be a classic Hel move, and I realized I'd been doing it way too much recently. Ransome probably thought I was some kind of hysterical maniac.

"You took ballet lessons as a kid?" he said.

For a second I was lost—could it be that I was being stalked by my stalkee? Then I realized I'd told him that on the hood of Buzz's car, when he'd so earnestly asked me about myself.

"Yeah," I answered, "when I was little."

I shouldn't have been amazed that Ransome had actually listened to what I'd said the other night—that's what we were supposed to expect, right? R-E-S-P-E-C-T and all that. Still, I was pleasantly surprised. Talking to John had always left me with the impression we were engaged in entirely different conversations. Me: "I'm trying to decide whether to apply to big colleges or small ones. What do you think?" John: "Uh-huh. You wanna watch a movie this weekend?" ("Watch a movie" was code for hook up in his parents' basement.) John hadn't even remembered my birthday. When he realized he'd forgotten it, he'd run to the Citgo a block from school on his free period and given me a gas-station rose in a cellophane cone as the final bell rang. So the fact that Ransome had retained this tiny, insignificant detail from my nervous ramblings about my childhood was pretty impressive. Maybe it was an age thing, I thought. Ransome was in college. Maybe they taught Listening to Girls 101 there (because guys obviously didn't get it in high school). Whatever it was, I liked it, and I wished Ransome hadn't moved to the other side of the hut.

"So are you still a dancer?" he asked.

I almost snorted I laughed so hard. "Ha! No. Katie Bell tells me I move like a one-armed sloth."

"Who's Katie Bell? Is that the redhead you always hang with?"

"Uh, yeah, she's my best friend." The words felt misshapen in my mouth, like square marbles. "She's"—I almost said "a camper"—"at camp."

A stitch of guilt, like when you tell someone you like her shirt but really you hate it, tugged at me, and I revised my explanation. I wasn't sure why I was hesitant to admit my best friend was younger. "She's still a cubby because her birthday's not until September. She shanked me during the cubby–counselor soccer game the other day."

I also wasn't sure why I threw in that last part, other than I'd found it pretty funny and thought Ransome might too.

He laughed. "She sounds like a spitfire."

"A spitfire?" Now I laughed. "You sound like a forty-year-old man!"

"Yeah. I should probably warn you that I'm kind of a dork."

"You're a dork? I guess we're well-suited to each other then."

Woops. Had I just said that? Too much? Was Ransome going to freak out that I'd already chosen the flowers for our wedding and named our three children? (In my defense, I *hadn't* gotten that far, although it *had* occurred to me how cool it would be to get married at camp, but that had been a long time ago.)

I started to do my awkward-silence-covering laugh, but Ransome said, "I guess so."

I was ready for him to kiss me right that minute—actually I'd been ready since I'd gotten out to the riflery range—but I had to wait a little while longer. It seemed like Ransome and I talked about anything and every-thing that night: our families, our friends from home, our campers, music, school. He was going back to

Tennessee as a sophomore in the fall. I asked him what college was like, and living with a roommate. Was it kind of like living in the cabins? No, he'd said as he laughed vaguely, it was different. He'd roomed with a friend from home, Billy. He was a Kappa Sig and played club rugby, which surprised me because, while Ransome was tall and definitely in shape, he didn't strike me as the football-without-pads type.

Finally he said, "Why don't you sit over here?"

I moved over to where he was sitting now with his back against the wall and his legs extended on the mattress. He rearranged so I could stretch out next to him and put his arm around me. We talked for a few more minutes, my heart knocking against my chest, until it got quiet and he finally leaned down and kissed me.

It was even better than the last time. It was better than any time. I'd done stuff *like* this before, but it was never like *this*. Ransome knew what he was doing in a way I now saw John, or any other guy I'd made out with for that matter, definitely had not.

At first I moved his hand when it searched my hip and moved down my leg, but it was a halfhearted, almost automatic reaction on my part. Of course I didn't want Ransome to think I was "that kind of girl," but I also didn't want him to stop. So half a minute later when his hand was there again, I let it stay until it wandered up to the button of my jeans. I fumbled for his.

When we were done hooking up, we were both quiet. My head was on his chest, and I was looking at a place on the wall where a camper named Amanda had signed her name next to the date, 1987. I was happy, really happy, but also worried that I hadn't been good at what we'd just done. I'd been to third base a few times before, with John. I didn't want to seem inexperienced, even if I was. Ransome's quietness worried me. I picked up my head and looked at his face. He looked over his nose at me and smiled.

"What?" he asked.

"Nothing. I can see up your nose," I observed, laughing at the awkward angle at which we were looking at each other.

"Nice," he said. "I hope I have some bats in the cave." He pinched his nostrils together with the hand that wasn't around me.

"Nope. All clear," I said, laying my head down again on his chest. I felt better. It was comfortable. Maybe I wasn't the best hookup Ransome had ever had, but I was lying here with him now, and it felt right. "I wish we could sleep here," I said drowsily. I had no idea what time it was, but I knew it was late.

"Me too," he said, and squeezed his arm tighter around my waist.

A few minutes later the bubble burst, and he said, "We should go. I don't want some poor Minnows stumbling on us in the morning and wondering why their counselors are half naked on top of each other at the riflery range."

"Years of therapy," I said. I knew we had to, but I was a little sad as we stood to go. I tugged my shirt on over my head as Ransome straightened the mattresses and checked for any stray cigarette butts. I stepped out of the hut into the moonlight and wrapped my arms around myself. The night was cold again.

Ransome followed me and wrapped his arms around me too. "I'll see you later?" he said.

I nodded, looking up at his face, and he kissed me.

"Okay," he said, as he released me. "Don't let the bed bugs bite."

I smiled and wanted to kiss him one more time, but didn't want to be the last to leave, so I said, "Okay," and turned to take the path back to my cabin. When I glanced over my shoulder, his back was retreating down the path to Brownstone. His hands were in his pockets, and I was in love. I sighed and smiled all the way back to my cabin. I could hardly believe this was real, but even if it was a dream, I didn't want to wake up.

Chapter 10

$\mathcal{I}$'ve always loved the saying "breaking bread together." It seems so simple but essential to bond over food. At camp, however, you didn't bond over dinner rolls; you bonded over pure, unadulterated sugar.

So I went, with a peace offering of Pixy Stix and two cans of Sun-Drop, to Katie Bell's cabin. I knew it was transparent, but I was ready to have my friend back. I *needed* my friend back.

The rain had held off for Field Day, allowing the Easts to beat the Wests, but descended with a vengeance the next afternoon. As we huddled in our bunks at rest hour, the clouds rolled in, bringing with them sheets of rain that swept like a curtain from one end of the valley to the other.

I, for one, loved rainy days at Southpoint. After a storm, a gauzy haze hung over the lake. Anything green suddenly perked up, and the air was thick with an earthy smell. But the life that suddenly saturated the outside world must have been sucked from the campers and counselors tucked in the cabins, because a lethargy overtook camp on afternoons like these. I wondered if everyone waited for the break the rain brought, like I did. Nothing could be expected of you in the rain.

Afternoon activities had been canceled until the weather cleared, which meant I wasn't expected on the swim dock, and could find Katie Bell sitting on her cabin porch. Her legs stretched across the stairs, she was flipping through a copy of *Star* magazine. She didn't see me as I walked up.

"Hey," I said. "What's going on?"

Katie Bell raised her chin and squinted against the hazy sunlight. "Not much. Just catching up on world events. I like to stay informed, ya know."

"Of course. . . . Hey, look what I got out of Cabin Six." I produced the bag of Pixy Stix, and Katie Bell smiled.

"And to wash them down . . ." I brought the two Sun-Drops, dangling from their plastic rings, from behind my back. Soft drinks, especially this super-sugary, highly caffeinated Tennessee specialty, were forbidden at camp. They had, therefore, developed into a kind of black-market currency, with counselors controlling the supply and campers the demand. They were usually only offered as payment for back massages or bribery.

"Sweet Mother of Sugar Shock," said Katie Bell, swinging her legs around and scooting over to make room for me on the step beside her. I sat and handed her one of the Sun-Drops.

"Don't tell anyone where you got it," I said as she popped the top and the soda gave a clean, satisfying hiss. "They'll be hounding me all day."

Katie Bell gulped down the electric-yellow liquid. She smacked her lips in sweet gratification. "Ahhhhhhh."

I ripped open the bag of Pixy Stix and offered Katie Bell a green one, her favorite color. We had had many arguments over whether the different color tubes were actually different flavors or just a trick of the mind. Without a word, she tore off the top, tilted her head back, and emptied an avalanche of sugar into her mouth.

"Oh, it's so good," she said, laughing and coughing at the same time, her eyes watering from the tartness.

My turn. This was how the game went until one or both of us got sick, or a counselor made us stop before we did. Now I was the counselor—no one to stop us. I slid a red stick from the bag, ripped it open, and emptied it down the hatch.

Squeezing my eyes shut, I shook my head. "Whoo!" I cried.

Katie Bell laughed, extracting a purple stick from the pack. "So," she said, "tell me about Ransome."

I was relieved that the Pixy Stix had worked their magic so quickly. I wiggled my toes. "What do you want to know?"

Katie Bell slapped at my leg. "Oh, come on, you tease! Spill it."

I grinned. "I don't know where to start! It was awesome." I'd been waiting to tell her every detail, but suddenly I felt shy.

"Start from the beginning," said Katie Bell, settling back against the steps to listen.

In a low voice, so that the girls napping or reading inside the cabin couldn't hear us, I told Katie Bell about our night off and how Ransome and I had sort of flirted, but how I'd been too nervous to *really* flirt. But then how, during the car ride, he'd surprised me by holding my hand. I told her about the overlook, where they'd taken us, and how Ransome and I had sat on the hood of the car talking—about real stuff—until he'd kissed me when I wasn't expecting it.

Katie Bell listened with an amused smile, lighting up at all the right parts, and when I got to the kiss, clapped her hands. "How was he? I mean as a kisser?"

My head fell back and I let out an amazed laugh. "Good." I blushed. "He was good. I mean, it was unexpected and quick because Winn turned, and I thought she saw us. . . ."

I stopped and wondered whether I should tell Katie Bell that Winn was acting strange. For a second I considered that I might just be paranoid, always looking for the gray cloud on the horizon. Besides, Katie Bell already didn't like Winn, and I still felt bad that I'd told Winn about the kiss before Katie Bell. But I was finally talking with my best friend again, and I wanted to tell her everything.

"You know," I started, my hands fidgeting nervously in my lap, "Winn's been acting kind of strange since that night. She's been kind of . . . mean."

Katie Bell looked thoughtful before saying, "That's weird. Why would—Oh my gosh! I totally forgot. Molly told me the other day, and I was going to tell you, but I forgot with Field Day, and then we were freaking out about the cubby show . . ."

I had a bad feeling. As Katie Bell rambled about all the reasons she'd forgotten to share what I suspected would not be good news, my stomach started to drop until I thought it might actually pass through my feet and land on the grass in front of us, a big pink blob. I just wanted Katie Bell to get to the point, and for it not to be something that would ruin the perfect summer I had already constructed in my head.

Finally she came around to it. "And Amanda heard from Lila that Winn's cubby year she used to sneak out with the counselors to the riflery range to meet Ransome. It was, like, top secret and super-scandalous when the older counselors found out. She might have even gotten in trouble with Fred." There was a hint, I thought, of satisfaction in Katie Bell's voice.

I wanted to throw up. How could I not have known?

"Are you sure? They hooked up?" I forced down a wave of nausea.

"That's what Molly said." The look on Katie Bell's face said she suddenly regretted telling me. "But that was two summers ago, Hel."

I nodded, my mind spinning as it tried to process the unwelcome information. I didn't want to think about Ransome hooking up with anyone, let alone my friend, to whom I'd recently spilled all about my crush.

Katie Bell kept talking. I wished she wouldn't. I wished she would just be quiet.

"Oh! And Molly also heard something else. . . . Did you know Abe's wife left him 'cause he was in love with Marjorie?!" Her eyes widened salaciously.

"That's not true," I shot. There was a sharpness in my voice I hadn't intended.

Immediately, Katie Bell went on the defensive. "I'm just telling you what I heard." The bag of Pixy Stix lay open and forgotten on the steps next to her. "Molly heard it from Amanda, who said Lila told her."

"Well, it's a rumor. Ransome told me so the other night, and I'd believe him over Molly." I hurled the words at her.

Ransome had confided in me. I knew how it felt to have people talking about you, pitying you behind your back, trading gossip, and all but salivating as they detailed the ways in which your family was crumbling around you. It felt like shit, and I didn't want Ransome to feel like shit. Ever. Even if he had hooked up with Winn two summers ago.

Katie Bell shrugged and stood, accidentally kicking the bag of Pixy Stix. The colorful paper tubes skittered over the steps and fell between the cracks.

"Sorry," she mumbled, but didn't bend to pick them up. "I'm just telling you what I heard, Helena."

I didn't answer, just stared at the ants already swarming over the candy.

"Thanks for the Sun-Drop," she said flatly. Then she disappeared into the cabin, still dark with its shutters closed against the rain.

I didn't bother to pick up the Pixy Stix. The ants would finish them off, or the rain, or other campers—I didn't care. I felt wretched from the sugar and the news, and suddenly all I wanted was the comfort of my bed.

My campers were out with Pookie playing in the creek, which had flooded with the rain, and I could have privacy there to hide under my covers and cry if I wanted.

What I'd come to repair with Katie Bell I'd only made worse, and what I'd come to share, I now wished I hadn't. What was happening between Ransome and me felt spoiled; the shine was taken out. I was glad I knew why Winn was acting so strange, but I had no idea how, or if, to confront her about it. I couldn't understand why she'd never said anything to me about Ransome, even when I'd told her I liked him. For the moment I'd just sleep, and pray for more rain.

The storm blew through, and we had a cool night followed by a scorching day. It was like the sun was trying to bake out of the ground every last drop of water, which we'd just gotten. At the swim dock, the campers could barely peel off their T-shirts and shorts fast enough to jump into the water.

For Winn, Sarah, and me, the heat was brutal. As lifeguards we were expected to stand vigilantly on the dock and were only allowed a dip in the lake between activity periods. By second activity, we'd all drained our water bottles, and not one of us was talking as we watched the girls splash and play.

Things with Winn had gone from bad to worse.

The times we had crossed paths in the few days since our night out—mainly on the swim dock and once accidentally in the Mess—she had looked past or through me. She only spoke when necessary and with a dismissiveness my mom would have called "sass." This made our mornings on the dock awkward at best and absolutely unbearable at certain moments, when I had to push my sunglasses down and stare out at the water to avoid crying.

I had decided not to say anything to Winn about Ransome. I could only imagine the mind-numbing awkwardness of that conversation.

At first I felt bad, wondering if I deserved Winn's anger. Then reason kicked in. I'd had no way of knowing about Winn and Ransome's secret past. She hadn't told me. Without Katie Bell—with whom I also wasn't speaking now—I still wouldn't know. That only confirmed my decision that the best thing to do was nothing at all. I was a pro at the path of least resistance. I only hoped if I ignored the situation, it would eventually go away.

In the meantime, I would try to weather Winn's sudden—and totally unfair, I sometimes wanted to shout—attitude. But what really worried me was whether Winn's being pissed might, or should, prevent me from going to the riflery range. Those late nights were my only chance to hang out with Ransome.

On the dock, my worry festered in the hot sun. It grew into panic, then indignation and, before I knew it, resentment at Winn's immaturity. I'd always looked up to her, I realized as I watched a camper do a back dive. First as my counselor and then as my friend, Winn had always seemed more grown-up, more experienced, cool. Not anymore. Now she just seemed petty and vindictive.

My mental reexamination of Winn's character was interrupted by a shrill blast from Sarah's whistle. The sound echoed off distant cliffs. Midway through every activity period, we were required to do a safety check, to make sure no one had drowned in the twenty minutes under our watch.

At the sound of the whistle, the girls climbed from the water and sat obediently on the main and floating docks. Routinely, they counted off—only this time, we came up short. There were nine Guppies and only eight voices that yelled out a number.

Winn and Sarah exchanged an anxious glance. The lake fell under an eerie silence. Even the water seemed to pause from its lapping against the dock. Again Sarah blew her whistle, and the girls counted off with more urgency this time.

"One."

"Two."

"Three."

"Four."

"Five.

"Six."

"Seven."

"Eight."

The silence that hung after "eight" was deafening.

There was a moment of paralyzed panic, and then Winn, Sarah, and I leaped into action. We ripped off our whistles and sunglasses and dove into the water. My heart was beating faster than the propeller of the boat I registered somewhere off in the distance.

We had a search protocol. I tagged the dock one arm's length from Sarah, who was one arm's length from Winn. In unison we took a gulp of air and plunged under water, sinking as fast as we could to the ice-cold bottom. When we felt nothing—not an arm or a leg or a torso, we kicked to the surface, moved forward one stroke, gasped another lungful of air, and descended again. This way, we worked in a slow fan across as much lake as three of us could cover. Every plunge brought the terror that I would be the one to feel the limp body, and every time my toes sunk into the freezing muck, it brought the other terror—that we wouldn't find her in time.

I heard the screaming as I was diving down for a

fourth time. There was a moment where my numb, confused brain didn't know whether to keep pushing for the bottom or swim for air and the voice that was trying to tell us something. I kicked wildly. When I broke the surface, I searched urgently for the source of the yelling. Lake water dripped into my eyes.

"It's Beth!" a camper on the dock was calling and pointing. The girl she pointed to was indeed Beth, a round, quiet girl who always, but especially now, looked bewildered. Beth was nearly tripping over her flip-flops as she hurried across the grassy area to the dock. She clutched her towel in a tight fist below her belly.

"What happened?" I gasped, swimming as fast as I could toward the dock.

Winn had already emerged, dripping, from the lake, and Sarah was climbing the ladder.

"Beth," Winn shouted, unloading on the poor girl the terror she had just felt as she searched for Beth's body in the cold, deep water, "where were you?"

Beth's lip trembled. "I, I had to the go the bathroom," she stammered. "I told Helena."

Winn turned her narrow-eyed glare on me; I was standing behind her on the dock, shivering with fear.

"Did she tell you she was going to the bathroom?" Winn asked. Her voice was as icy as the muck at the bottom of the lake.

"No," I said, shaking my head, looking between Beth and Winn. "Really, if she did, I didn't hear her." I was telling the truth.

Winn's blue eyes locked on to mine. "This isn't a joke, Helena. Someone could die out here."

Behind Winn, Beth's lip began to tremble. "I, I'm sorry," she said behind watery eyes. "I thought I told her. . . ."

"Beth," said Sarah, stern but gentle, "you know what you have to do."

"Yeah." Beth's voice wavered. Slowly, she dropped her towel and backed off the dock, where she sat cross-legged and dejected on the bare, prickly grass. It was our standard punishment for not taking swim check seriously.

Winn looked at me as if she was going to say something. I wondered if she wanted me on the prickly grass as well. Instead she turned and climbed, without a word, to the top of the lifeguard stand.

"Okay," she shouted to the rest of the campers, who were watching Beth's punishment with mixed sympathy and cruel pleasure. "Show's over. If anyone else wants to go to the bathroom, ask me or Sarah."

Winn raised the plastic whistle to her lips and blasted a long high note, and the Guppies, except for Beth, dove back into the cool water.

Chapter 11

We didn't exactly *need* a counselor by the lemonade table at the dance—how hard is it to pour yourself a paper cup of lemonade?—but I volunteered for the post anyway. The truth was, I wasn't sure where else to stand.

Katie Bell was dancing with her friends from Cabin Nine on the far side of the tennis courts. They'd even opened the circle to allow in a few brave Brownies. She hadn't spoken to me since our spat on her cabin steps. Maybe I'd overreacted, but somehow it still rankled, the way she'd told me about Winn and Ransome. Had I caught that glimmer of satisfaction in her eyes as she'd said it? Or was I just revising history? Either way, it didn't change that we weren't talking.

Neither were Winn and I—at all now. In what I assumed was a show of solidarity, even Sarah and

Lizbeth were keeping their distance from me. If it hadn't been for Pookie's company at our Mess table—and Ransome—I don't know what I would have done. Every day I counted the hours until I could see him.

Despite the knots of dread in my stomach, I'd been out to the riflery range the past two nights. Both times Ransome had been the only one to say anything more than "hi" to me. In the corner, we'd talked quietly. Conversation poured out of us easily now. In a way, I had known Ransome forever (at least since I was nine), but not the *real* Ransome. *Him* I was just getting to know. And I wanted to know everything.

Both nights, Ransome and I had waited until everyone else wandered back to the cabins and we were the only ones left. I knew the other counselors were talking about us, but I didn't care.

We'd stretched out on the musty mattresses with the stuffing coming out and buttons poking into our backs, and talked and made out until streaks of orange and pink showed in the sky.

Thinking about it even now, at the dance, made me flushed. Embarrassed, as if any bystander could read my thoughts, I over-helped an awkward Brownstone camper with glasses and too-short shorts who was fumbling with the lemonade spout.

"Thanks," he said suspiciously, taking the cup from

my hand and trundling back to his friends.

I surveyed the tennis court. Winn was on the bleachers, surrounded by the usual counselors and some Brownies, but Ransome was still nowhere to be found. I hadn't seen him at the cookout, where I'd eaten my hamburger seated cross-legged on the ground with Ruby and Melanie. Ruby had cracked me up when she asked if Melanie wanted a "pressure burger" and, when Melanie said yes, picked up her burger and squished it between her two small hands until it was as flat as a pancake. "Enjoy your pressure burger." She'd grinned triumphantly as she deposited the squashed sandwich back on Melanie's plate.

Suddenly, two large hands covered my eyes from behind. Before he said anything, I knew it was Ransome. I would recognize his smell anywhere. I caught whiffs of him during the day after the nights we spent together, and it made me dizzy.

I laughed and turned, prying his hands free of my face.

"Hey," he said, grinning in the irresistible way that made even my worst mood dissolve like sugar in water.

"Hey yourself."

"Manning the lemonade stand?"

"Looks like it."

"Well," Ransome grunted, squinting and posing like

John Wayne (sometimes he *was* a forty-year-old man), "it's a tough job, but someone's got to do it." It was dorky and cheesy and adorable. And I laughed.

"Where have you been?" I asked.

"A kid in my cabin's homesick. I had to help Dad . . . Abe, talk him down from the ledge."

I frowned. "Is he okay now?"

"Yeah." Ransome looked unconcerned. I guessed the way they dealt with homesickness at Brownstone was a little different from how we handled it at Southpoint, with lots of hugs and positive reinforcement. Although, not that many campers at Southpoint got homesick, especially after the first few days. More often, we got campsick when we went home.

"Hey," Ransome said quietly, looking out over the tennis court but speaking to me, "I was thinking . . . if things seem to be under control here," he joked, gesturing toward the cooler, "maybe you could sneak away and meet me at the barn." His eyes met mine. I was expecting them to be confident and cool, but they weren't, which comforted me because I wasn't either. We'd hooked up almost every night that week, but I still got butterflies like I wasn't sure it was going to happen again.

"Unless you think things will get crazy at the lemonade stand in your absence," he said.

"Shut up." I smiled, and my heart beat like a trapped bird in my chest. "Okay."

I'd never snuck away from a dance before. I knew some people did, once it got dark, but only behind the Mess or even just outside the circles of the tennis court lights. Never to the barn—it was almost on the other side of camp.

"Okay," said Ransome. "I'll meet you there in . . . fifteen minutes?"

I smiled, the flush rising again from my toes and spreading through my body to my cheeks. "Yeah," I said. "I'll see you there."

Not to raise suspicion, I had walked first to the Bath, where I quickly brushed my teeth and washed my hands. Then I'd continued purposefully toward the cabins, so that if anyone asked, I could say I was going to get a sweater from my trunk, before cutting in a wide arc past the softball diamond and up toward the barn. I knew I was being ridiculous taking the long way, but if someone caught me, maybe another counselor who had snuck away for a cigarette, I had no idea how I'd explain myself.

Thanks to my detours, I had to hurry, so I was sweating slightly by the time I reached the paddock in front of the barn. A thin layer of perspiration beaded on my upper lip, and I wiped at it with the back of my wrist before I unlatched the gate that kept the horses from escaping. The hinge creaked as I closed it behind me.

I was looking for Ransome but didn't see him. I thought about calling his name but didn't, irrationally afraid someone from the dance might hear me. Carefully, I picked a clear path through the manure minefields that dotted the paddock.

"Hey."

I jumped when I heard him. "You scared me!"

Ransome came out from the barn. He laughed, resting his hand on my back. It was a casual gesture on his part, but I was still keenly aware of these things.

"Sorry." He smiled. "Didn't mean to . . . Come here; I want you to meet someone."

I followed him into the barn and down the center aisle of the stables. From their stalls, the horses watched us with gleaming, dark eyes. Some pawed at the floor with a hoof, or rocked from one front leg to the other, as if they were either bored or ready to bolt. The smell of the barn reminded me unmistakably of Southpoint. Unlike Katie Bell, I rode only at camp, but I loved it. I'd sometimes come out here with her at free periods to walk and trot on the old nags while she practiced her jumping.

Stopping in front of a stall almost at the end of the

aisle, Ransome swung open the half door and stepped inside. I followed him in. At the back of the stall was a horse I'd never seen before. She was a beautiful chestnut color with a white diamond on her nose.

"This," said Ransome, rubbing the ridge of her nose from the tuft of mane between her ears down to her flared nostrils, "is Penny. We just got her."

As I brushed my fingers over the white diamond, Penny closed her eyes. Her eyelashes were incredibly long and flirtatious.

"Hey, Penny," I said softly. I ran my hand down her strong neck to her flank. She exhaled loudly and stomped one of her hooves. "She's a sweetie."

"She is."

Ransome was standing behind me now. He reached his hand over my shoulder to pat Penny on her side. He was so close, my breath caught in my throat. Holding it, I turned. Closemouthed, he smiled back at me. There was a single fleck of green in his right eye that I hadn't noticed before.

I wanted him to kiss me so bad it hurt. It was scrambling my brain. Instead, he walked once more around Penny, then out of the stall. He waited for me to follow, then closed the door behind us.

"So, Helena," he said, interlacing his fingers behind the small of my back.

"So, Ransome . . ." I teased. I locked my arms around his waist and leaned back to look up at him, so that our lower bodies pressed into each other. I smiled like I had a secret.

He laughed.

"What are you laughing at?" I protested.

"You," he said, and finally lowered his face to mine.

Pushed against the barn wall, we kissed like this for a few minutes before I got nervous.

Reluctantly pulling away, I bit my lip. "What if someone notices we're gone and comes looking for us?"

Being caught by Fred would be worse than being caught by your parents. The sun was sinking lower in the sky, and I didn't want to be away from the dance past dark.

"They won't," Ransome assured me, his mouth brushing the side of my face and neck.

It tickled and I reflexively pushed my ear to my shoulder and laughed. "But what if they do?"

"In the barn?" he asked, looking at me earnestly.

I didn't reply.

"Come on." He stepped back and gently pulled me by the hand. "I know where we can go."

In the corner of the building, where a few pitchforks and shovels were stacked against the wall, a ladder ascended through a small square hole in the ceiling. Ransome released my hand and started to climb up.

"Where are we going?" I asked, gazing up after him.

"The hayloft," his voice answered from above.

Cautiously, I scaled each rung, realizing it wasn't the best time to be wearing flip-flops. When I emerged on the other side of the opening, it was dark and about ten degrees warmer. Hay bales were stacked along the walls. A few had tipped over and were resting at haphazard angles.

Throwing his weight against it, Ransome pushed open the sliding panel that covered a small window to let in some air and light. My eyes adjusted, and I saw mouse droppings and bird poop nearly covering the floor. A sooty lantern dangled from the center of the ceiling. It looked as if it hadn't been used in quite awhile.

"Are there mice up here?" I asked, trying to sound like I didn't care one way or the other.

"Yeah, but they won't bother us."

I looked around for someplace to sit, but nowhere looked inviting. I wasn't so sure about this.

Catching the hesitant look on my face, Ransome said, "Hang on a sec," and descended the ladder. When he came back he was carrying a clean, blue, wool horse blanket. He laid it across a few of the hay bales.

"This okay?" he asked. "If not, we can—"

"Sure," I said quickly, and sat down next to him on the blanket.

In a second we were kissing again, and before long had lain down across the makeshift bed. Ransome's hand wandered over my jeans and between my legs. But the hay was poking into my back, and suddenly all I could think about was Winn.

I had decided not to say anything to either Winn or Ransome about what Katie Bell had told me, but in the dim shelter of the hayloft, my plan went out the small square window. As Ransome kissed my ear, I put my hand against his chest and pushed gently.

"Ransome," I whispered.

"Huh?" he mumbled, nuzzling against my neck.

"Ransome," I said again, pushing harder.

He pulled away, realizing I was actually saying something. "Yeah?" An unreadable shadow crossed his face.

"Can I ask you something?" I squirmed awkwardly under him.

"Of course." He propped himself on one elbow. "What's up?" I could almost see all the things he was worried I was going to say cross his mind in rapid succession.

"Nothing," I lied, melting again at the concern on his face and wishing I hadn't brought it up. "It's not a big deal . . . I just . . . I heard something the other day and . . . I just need to know."

"Okay . . ."

"I heard . . ." I bit my bottom lip. "Did you and Winn used to hook up?"

Ransome rolled his eyes and hung his head close to my chest.

"I mean, it's not a big deal if you did," I said quickly. "That was a while ago, before us—I mean, not that there's an us, but . . ." I faded off, wondering if I'd said too much.

Ransome smiled reassuringly, like he suddenly understood, like he could read my thoughts. "There is an 'us,' at least according to me . . . and I've never hooked up with Winn."

The grapefruit-size knot in my stomach relaxed. "Are you sure?"

He laughed. "Of course I'm sure. I like to think I'm a stud, but it's not like I've hooked up with so many girls I can't remember!"

I smiled and rolled my eyes. "I just want to make sure I haven't given Winn a reason to hate me, like hooking up with her ex or something."

"No," said Ransome, sitting up and straightening his shirt. "Two years ago, when Winn was still a camper, she had some crazy crush on me." *Note to self: Never tell Ransome about your crazy camper crush.* "She was friends with some older counselors, and they brought her out to the riflery range a couple times. She thought she was gonna hook up with me, but we never did. I would never hook up with a camper . . . or Winn, for that matter."

I nodded. "Okay. I just needed to know, because Winn's been acting strange."

"Well, I don't know who told you that, but Winn is definitely not my 'ex,' and she has no reason to be pissed at you."

I was relieved. I nodded again and suddenly wanted the conversation to be over. Sitting up, I kissed him and wrapped my arms around his neck. Both of us grinning, I pulled Ransome's body on top of mine.

It happened faster than I'd always thought it would. I'm still not sure of the whole sequence of events, only that one minute Ransome and I were making out like we had half a dozen times before, and the next . . .

He had pulled off my shirt first and then his own as I wiggled out of my jeans and unbuckled his belt. He tugged at my underwear, and suddenly we were naked against each other.

I'm pretty sure I whispered, "Wait."

Ransome paused, his body hovering over mine,

every muscle in his arms and shoulders tensed, his weight supported on his hands on either side of my head.

"You don't want to?" he asked breathlessly. My mind raced along his words, trying to gauge what lay behind them.

"No, it's just that . . ." I did want to. Every molecule of my body was screaming like it was on fire, and the only thing to put the fire out was to give in.

He pressed down and against me, closer this time to the place where I knew there was no going back.

"Do you want to?" he asked again. There was an urgency, almost a desperation in his voice, but he wasn't pleading, he was asking. If I had said no, he would have stopped.

So I said yes.

"Do we need a . . . ?"

"Yeah." He reached up to his pants, which he'd thrown over a hay bale behind us. From the pocket he pulled a blue foil square. He fumbled until finally he ripped open the corner with his teeth and produced an innocent-looking circle of off-white latex.

I realized I was holding my breath as he unrolled the condom with one hand. When it was on, he looked into my eyes. "You're sure?"

I nodded. Ransome kissed me. I thought, This is it, and very slowly, he pushed into me.

Instantly a blunt pain ripped through my abdomen. For a second I panicked, thinking maybe he'd done something wrong. My friend Lindsay, from home, had told me the first time was bad, but was it supposed to hurt like this? It didn't look like it in the movies. No one ever curled up in the fetal position out of searing pain in the middle of a sex scene.

Noticing me wince, Ransome looked concerned and quickly backed off. "It's okay," I whispered, and then, slower this time, he pushed into me again. His eyes were closed like he was concentrating very intently. This time hurt, but not as much. When he pulled out again, I looked down. I was bleeding.

"Are you okay?" he asked, alarmed.

"Yeah," I assured, though I was slightly alarmed at the sight myself. I was mortified but tried to smile. "It's okay."

Behind his green-flecked eyes, Ransome wavered, as if he too was just understanding what we were actually doing. Then the hesitation vanished, and he kissed me and continued moving above me. He rocked gently at first and then harder until his skin was damp and he was breathing hard, like the horses in the stalls below us. I tried to close my eyes, like you were supposed to, but I couldn't. I wanted to watch him. His eyes were shut tight, but his mouth hung slightly open so that I could see the tips of his teeth. I wasn't sure why, but I focused on these—his white teeth, one turned slightly inward, as if pushed out of line by the others. Bully teeth.

Ransome's pace quickened until finally his eyes squeezed tighter, his face twisted, and he shuddered and let out a tiny groan. Exhausted, he dropped his weight across my chest, the only thing between us a layer of sweat. His rib cage heaved up and down.

Not knowing what to say or where to look, I stared at the lantern suspended from the ceiling and noticed an abandoned nest that some bird had painstakingly made in its glass hollow.

I ran my hand down Ransome's warm back, my fingertips sticking to his skin.

Finally he lifted himself off me and rolled over. The condom, which had looked equal parts innocent and intimidating before, looked almost comical now.

"I'm sorry, Hel," he said, still short of breath. "I didn't know it was your first time. I wouldn't have—"

"You wouldn't have?" I asked, not accusing but worried.

"I mean, I just would have . . . made it nicer."

I rolled over and kissed him lightly on the lips. "It was nice," I said. I felt like that was the kind of thing I was supposed to say.

The truth was that I felt as if I'd been ripped in two. I couldn't go back to the dance like this. I'd have to go to my cabin and change, maybe stay in my bed and pretend like I'd gotten my period and didn't feel well.

Ransome extended his arm, and I cradled my head in the space where his chest met his shoulder. He kissed the top of my head and inhaled the smell of my hair. "It was nice," he agreed. "I hope it was for you."

I nodded against his shoulder. "It was."

But a hiccup of panic had suddenly risen in my chest. I had done it. I was no longer a virgin. When I'd followed Ransome up the ladder to the hayloft, I'd had no intention of having sex for the first time, no premonition that I was about to make a decision I would carry with me for the rest of my life. I'd had no idea that Ransome would be my first. Or had I? Had I known all along?

I'd wanted to do it, I reminded myself. I'd made the choice and said yes for a reason. Because I cared about Ransome—maybe, probably, loved him—and it wasn't about how or where or when; it was about who. I told myself all these things because I couldn't believe what had just happened. It had taken maybe ten minutes. Ten minutes to lose my virginity. Though that was a weird turn of phrase. I hadn't lost anything; I'd given it up.

Nervous that I wasn't saying anything, Ransome gently stroked my arm and the outside of my hip with his fingertips. "Are you okay?" he asked.

I snuggled against him, inhaling his scent—that mixture of deodorant and sweat that mingled with the musty-sweet smell of the hay, and for the second time that evening, as I watched the sun dip below the tree line through the barn's high window, I said yes. For the second time that night, I was three-quarters of the way sure I meant it.

Taps

The weathered wood grabs at my bathing suit. The hot sun dried it quickly, except for my butt, which leaves a heart-shaped stamp when I stand. Walking to the edge of the dock, I curl my toes over the rough planks. The sun throws rays of light like arrows into the green water. It laps at the algae-slick posts of the ladder, also at the sailboats and motorboats tethered to the dock farther down the shore.

The diving board scratches like sandpaper on my bare feet, but it's loose and springy, the way I like. It makes me wobbly in the knees. I jump to the sky, float in midair like a bird flying against the wind, then splash down down down into the black, like a rock. The skin of the water is warm, but deeper it's almost freezing, curling around my calves with icy fingers. When I touch bottom, the muck is silky soft between my toes. There is a moment, eyes closed, hair swirling around my neck, time suspended, when I wonder what would happen if I didn't rise again to the surface. But my lungs are starting to burn, so I kick and break through the surface with a gasp.

Chapter 12

I was one of the first out to the flagpole after Reveille blew the next morning. I hadn't slept very soundly, tossing and turning all night from strange dreams that didn't make sense but felt incredibly real. I was snorkeling in an ocean teeming with sharks and octopuses. In real life I'd never even snorkeled before. The closest I'd gotten to that kind of sea life was the Chattanooga aquarium.

When I woke up, and even after I'd wrapped myself in a blanket and tromped outside to stand at the flagpole, I was drowsy and discombobulated. The night before—the dance, the hayloft—still felt oddly hazy. That's why I couldn't make sense at first of what Pookie was saying to me.

"They pulled it off," she whispered excitedly.

I looked at her, wondering if I was still dreaming. "Pulled what off?"

"Last night they put Buzz's and Ransome's beds on the floating dock while everyone was at the dance. Wasn't it your idea?" she said, as if I should have known.

Some of the fog lifted, and I realized that the other counselors had pulled off my prank. "Who did it?" I asked, already able to guess.

"I think Winn and Lizbeth and Sarah and Caroline. There was a group of them. The rest of us had to stay here so the guys wouldn't get suspicious." Maybe because of the confused and disappointed look on my face, Pookie added, "They looked for you before they went over, but Winn said they couldn't find you anywhere."

I nodded, wrapping my blanket tighter and looking over at Winn, who'd joined her campers at the flagpole. She'd pulled my prank without me. Or was it my fault for missing it by sneaking off to have sex with Ransome in the hayloft? For a second I was scared Pookie would ask where I'd been when they couldn't find me. I'd never been a good liar, especially not at eight o'clock in the morning.

Luckily she didn't, and "Oh" was all I said.

Winn caught me staring. For a second we held each other's gaze before she looked away. Lizbeth had come up beside her and said something quietly. I figured it was about the prank because Winn nodded and laughed, and two of the campers next to her giggled with wide-eyed amazement. They looked up at their counselor adoringly. Winn put a finger to her lips to signal them to be quiet as Butter bounded up to the flagpole.

"Good morning!" Marjorie called, and Winn's campers quickly stood at attention.

I was sad and angry for missing the prank I'd planned myself; but angry with whom—myself or Winn—I wasn't quite sure.

I had been left behind, like dead weight. When Winn and the other girls took their night off the third week, they signed up with Caroline, who was twenty-two and could buy them Boone's Farm at the Wal-Mart on the edge of town. Only four counselors could leave the camp grounds at a time. I knew that. We all knew that.

With the way Winn had been acting—alternating between completely ignoring me and skewering me with passive-aggressive comments about small things like forgetting to sweep under my Mess table or being the last counselor to the dock—I was fine with this scenario. I proved it by volunteering to be COD, as if this had been my Monday night plan all along.

Besides, I still hadn't wrapped my head around what had happened—what *was* happening—with Ransome. We'd met again Sunday night at the riflery range, even though most of the other counselors had stayed in. We'd talked and fooled around but kept it strictly PG. But while staying up with Ransome until sunrise was all I wanted to do, it was seriously cutting into my sleep time. When he wasn't around, the adrenaline rush wore off, and I was sluggish and tired. A quiet night in the cabin as COD, followed by a good night's sleep, sounded like a great idea.

After Evening Gathering and the get-ready-for-bed call of Tattoo, I watched my campers shuffle and knock around the cabin in the soft lantern light. They dragged out trunks, put away flashlights and sweatshirts, and searched for pajamas and stuffed animals that had fallen in the cracks between their bunks and the wall.

Evening Gathering had been a bonfire and ghost story. When Fred reached the part where the ghoulish, bloodthirsty mountain man is discovered roaming through the cabins at night, the girls had shuddered and huddled closer together. At the climax, when Fred shined his flashlight into the ghoul's two . . . red . . . *EYES*, there had been a collective bloodcurdling scream. Even I jumped. No matter how many times I heard Fred tell the story, it still scared the bejeezus out of me.

The effect of ghost-story nights was that it took the camp much longer to settle down for bed. There were the inevitable pranksters who liked to jump out from behind the Bath or cabins, sending the girls shrieking and running in every direction. The campers did everything in pairs after a ghost story, and they made sure to make lots of noise as they did it.

As the youngest, my campers seemed especially agitated. I had to push and prod them into their pajamas and finally their beds, where they were supposed to be at the sound of Taps, the magical bugle call that immediately silenced even the loudest, shrieking-est of girls.

The first plaintive note blasted from the direction of the Mansion. I quickly extinguished the lantern, and miraculously, in seconds, all my girls were in their beds and quiet, not a trace of the rowdy bunch they'd been moments before. The entire camp listened reverently as Fred bugled the good-night song—more a salute to the day than a lullaby. When he was done, you could have heard a pin drop on the cabin floor.

"Should I read tonight?" I asked. "Or have y'all had enough stories for one evening?"

"Yes! Yes!" a few girls pleaded from their beds. "Another chapter!"

I got up and and shuffled to my cubby for the dog-eared copy of *Harry Potter*. We would never finish it before the end of camp, but the girls begged me to read it every night. It was our ritual and possibly, apart from my time at the riflery range with Ransome, my favorite part of the day. I think the steady hum of my voice as it drifted over the printed words comforted me as much as it did them.

Settling back on my bed, the book cradled in my lap and my flashlight propped on the ledge above my head, I began. "Chapter Eight."

"Helena?" A soft voice came out of the darkness before I could get to Harry and Hogwarts.

"Yeah, Ruby?"

"Can I sit in your lap while you read?"

I never wanted to play favorites, but secretly I adored Ruby. At the bonfire she'd cowered in my lap and squeezed my hand tight when Fred shouted at the end of his story. She hadn't cried, but she'd been unusually quiet as she prepared for bed, and I knew she was scared.

"Sure," I answered. "Just until we're done reading. Then you need to go back to your bed."

Ruby quickly found her place in my lap. Her head fit perfectly under my chin, and I couldn't help but miss having a lap to crawl into when I was frightened and cold.

Sighing, I continued. "Chapter Eight . . ."

I had read two chapters by the time Ruby's head started to droop and the breathing of the girls drew out into long, exhausted snores.

"Ruby," I whispered, clicking off the flashlight. "Time to get in your bed."

Half asleep, she rubbed at her face and swayed back to her bunk, where her eyes closed before she'd even collapsed. I pulled the covers over her and climbed into my own bed. As COD, I was supposed to stay awake for a while, in case someone got sick or scared (likely tonight) and needed to go to the Mansion, but I didn't feel like reading anymore. Instead I lay there in the dark, listening to the girls' steady breathing and the chorus of frogs down at the lake. Behind the frogs was the high-pitched constant screech of the cicadas.

Eventually, inevitably, my thoughts drifted to Ransome. Remembering the night in the hayloft flipped my stomach upside down and tightened my chest. I knew, if I was being honest, that a gnawing fear of regret—not regret itself, but *fear of regret*—had begun to creep into my thoughts of Ransome. I wanted to be happy with my decision, and I was, I repeated over and over. Ransome and I were meant to be together. This wasn't just a silly camp hookup, like Sarah and Buzz. This was real. There was nothing to feel bad about.

Still, I was a jumble of thoughts and emotions. I wanted to tell Katie Bell that I had lost my virginity to Ransome, but I hadn't begun to work up the guts. I wasn't sure when, or if, I would.

It wasn't that Katie Bell and I weren't just getting along—we'd been in fights before, even stopped speaking for days—it was that we weren't even existing on the same *plane* anymore. Katie Bell was still a camper. She couldn't understand how things could change—and so quickly.

I found myself suddenly jealous of the time when things were simple, when days centered on creek walks and tetherball, and your biggest worry was whether you'd have riding or sailing. There were no boys, there were no secrets or rumors, and there were no regrets. Not even fear of regret. There was just a best friend and endless hours to fill with Pixy Stix and laughing so hard you couldn't breathe.

Tears were spilling from the corners of my eyes before I knew they were coming. Afraid that my campers would hear me, I rolled over and buried my face in the pillow. It smelled like camp, which made me cry harder. A dam broke inside of me, like when it rained for a few days and the lake flooded and ran over the old water spill. I cried like that until I drifted off into an exhausted sleep.

When the beam of the flashlight hit my face, my first thought was that a camper was sick, and as COD I needed to get her down to the Mansion. The bright light and harsh whispers shot me up out of my stonelike sleep.

"Helena . . . Helena . . . wake up," a familiar voice hissed.

I propped myself on an elbow and squinted at the person behind the flashlight. Slowly my brain focused, and with a sinking sensation, I knew who it was standing over my bed. It wasn't the other COD or a sick camper; it was Winn.

"What's wrong?" I asked.

"I need to talk to you."

"Now?"

"Now."

"Okay . . . where? Can you turn your flashlight off? I don't want to wake up my campers."

The flashlight clicked off, and it was black again, except for the light from the Bath filtering through the cabin windows.

"Meet us at the softball diamond."

Abruptly, Winn and the figure behind her, who I could now identify as Sarah, left the cabin. I sat up, fully awake and suddenly feeling as if *I* needed to be taken to the Mansion for medical treatment.

Why would Winn wake me like the gestapo in the middle of the night? Shivering, I slipped on my tennis shoes and wrapped my blanket around my shoulders.

I checked the beds to make sure none of the girls had woken up, and trudged toward the softball diamond.

Whatever Winn had to talk about, the tone of her voice told me it wasn't good, and I had one educated guess who it might involve. Suddenly I was seized with a cold panic that Winn knew where I had been the other night; she knew what Ransome and I had done in the hayloft. Had he told people? Had someone seen us? Could she read it on my face, like I sometimes imagined people could when you lost your virginity? I wanted to throw up.

When I arrived, Winn and Sarah were already sitting on the bleachers. "Hi," I said meekly, before taking a seat on the bench below them.

Winn pounced. "Where do you get off, Helena?" I'd heard the expression "spitting mad" before, but I'd never actually seen someone so pissed I was afraid she might really spit on me. Until now.

"What do you mean?" I was astonished by the force of her anger.

"I thought we were friends, but I don't talk behind my friends' backs."

"I don't either," I protested.

Sarah inhaled and made a face that suggested otherwise.

"Really?" Winn's narrowed eyes continued to dig into me. "Then why did Ransome accuse me tonight of telling you that we hooked up? We didn't hook up. And I didn't tell you that. So forgive me if I was slightly embarrassed trying to convince him of that after you told him I said it."

I was speechless and numb. I had never intended for Ransome to say something to Winn.

"I . . . I . . ." I stuttered unconvincingly, "didn't tell Ransome that you said—"

"So Ransome's lying?" Sarah interrupted. Now it was obvious her reason for coming—bitchery in numbers.

"No!" I backtracked quickly. "I mean, I did ask him if y'all had hooked up, but I didn't say that you'd told me that. He misunderstood. . . . I'd heard from Katie Bell that you used to sneak out to meet him when you were a cubby, and . . ."

I couldn't see much in the dark, but I caught Winn stiffen.

"Katie Bell told you that?" Her voice was scarily measured. "How would Katie Bell know what I was and wasn't doing when I was a cubby? She was, like, ten then." That was an exaggeration, but I didn't argue.

"I don't know," I stammered. I was suddenly very confused. I just wanted to go back to bed. "I'm sorry, Winn. The only reason I asked Ransome was because you'd been acting mad at me since our night out. I didn't want to step on your toes if you and Ransome had some sort of . . . history. You hadn't said anything, but then Katie Bell heard it, and it made sense that maybe you were mad, but I didn't know—"

"Well, we don't have 'history,'" snapped Winn. "And I'd appreciate it if you and your little friend would keep your rumors to yourselves. Come on," she said to Sarah.

Without giving me another glance, Winn and Sarah stomped off the bleachers and back to the cabins.

Even though the refuge of my bed was all I wanted, I couldn't find the energy to rise from the cold metal bench just yet. I stayed at the softball diamond a while longer and, pulling my blanket around me tighter, cried beneath the open sky.

Chapter 13

Ruby nestled in her usual place on my lap as Skit Night unfolded on the Bowl's stage. At the moment, Table Twelve was staging a Southpoint version of *Saturday Night Live*'s "Weekend Update." The "anchors" were two campers pretending to be Fred and Marjorie, reporting on such sensational stories as the toilets in the Bath clogging from campers using too much toilet paper, and a report from the "foreign" correspondent at Brownstone on the budding romance between Sarah and a certain male counselor whose name rhymed with "fuzz." The counselors and older campers who got the joke turned to Sarah, who blushed and buried her face in a laughing Winn's shoulder. Considering the previous night's blowout with Winn, I was relieved the kids hadn't caught wind of Ransome and me—yet, at least.

Ruby had leaned back to ask loudly what everyone was laughing about, when Katie Bell crept up and hunched down next to me.

"I need to talk to you." Her voice was urgent, with hard edges. It was like dejá-vù. It seemed the only reason anyone needed to talk to me now was to pick a fight.

"About what?" I whispered uneasily.

Katie Bell glanced at Ruby, who was looking between my bewildered face and Katie Bell's glowering one. "Do you really want me to say it here?"

"Ruby," I said quietly, sliding her off my lap, "I'll be right back."

"Nooo," Ruby started to protest, but I hushed her and pointed at the stage.

"I'll be right back."

Silently I followed Katie Bell up the path from the Bowl to the Mansion in the lowering dusk. She held her body taut and clenched. Not once did she turn to look at me. When we reached the Yard, I thought she would go to sit in one of the white Adirondack chairs, but instead, Katie Bell spun around to fix me with a fierce stare.

"Why did you tell Winn I told you about her and Ransome?" she demanded.

My face felt weirdly numb as I realized, with a sinking heart, that I wasn't the only one Winn had paid a visit to the night before.

"Katie Bell, I'm sorry . . . I didn't mean to tell her. It just came out." The corners of Katie Bell's mouth turned down in a scowl. "I wasn't going to say anything to Ransome—I was just going to let it go—but then it slipped out the other night when . . . He must have said something to Winn. Did she come to your cabin last night? I think maybe she'd been—"

"No." Katie Bell cut me off. "She cornered me today at afternoon activities and bitched me out in front of Molly and Amanda. . . . How could you tell on me to Winn like that? You're supposed to be my best friend!"

"I didn't! I am!" I protested. "Winn cornered me too. She came to my cabin last night and woke me up, dragged me out to the softball diamond."

Katie Bell's eyes were suddenly brimming. A single tear slid down the side of her nose, glistening over her freckles. She quickly pawed it away, her hands returning to her sides in two white-knuckled fists.

"You don't even talk to me anymore!" she exploded. "You're too busy trying to be, like"—she struggled for the words—"cool Counselor Helena, working on the swim dock and hanging out with Winn and sticking your tongue down Ransome's stupid throat, to think about the 'little people.'" She made air quotes to exaggerate the ridiculousness of the term.

"That is not true, Katie Bell." Tears were stinging my eyes now too. "Stop blaming me for something that's not my fault. I can't help it that you're three months younger than I am. I can't help it that Fred wouldn't let you be a counselor. And I can't help it that I've grown up and you haven't!" I hadn't meant to, but I realized I was shouting.

Katie Bell's eyes narrowed to two dark slits. "Oh, you think you're grown-up?" she said in a quiet, controlled voice that was bursting at the seams with rage. "Well, if ditching your best friend is grown-up, then I don't mind being a kid."

Back at the Bowl I could hear clapping and the singing of camp songs. The darkness had wrapped itself around us now, obscuring Katie Bell and me from one another. A mass of silence stood between us.

"Fine," I said, not sure what I was confirming or rejecting with this word, but that it was the only way I knew to end an argument I didn't want to be having.

"Fine," said Katie Bell, and stalked off in the direction of the Bath.

I couldn't follow her there, and I didn't want to go back to the Bowl yet, so I instead made a beeline for the Mansion. The screen door slammed behind me.

"Helena?" Marjorie's voice said.

Startled, I turned to find her standing in the

front hall. I quickly wiped the tears from my cheeks and tried to act casual.

"Hi, Marjorie. Sorry, I needed to use the bathroom."

Technically we weren't supposed to use the bathrooms in the Mansion. The plumbing was old and couldn't handle a hundred girls who didn't feel like walking all the way to the Bath. But it was the best I could come up with while trying not to cry.

"Okay," Marjorie said hesitantly. "Honey, are you okay?" She put the papers she was holding on a table and came toward me. "Is everything all right?"

It wasn't, and I wanted to tell her that. Instead I squeaked, "Yeah."

Marjorie wasn't buying it, I could tell, but she nodded. Without asking more, she put her arms around me in a hug. I closed my eyes against her shoulder—I hadn't realized until now that I had grown taller than her.

"This is a hard time, isn't it?" she said. I nodded, my breath catching in my throat as I tried to stop crying.

Marjorie was quiet for a second, then pulled away, still holding my shoulders. "You remember how a few years ago we had those seventeen-year cicadas?" she said. "They left their shells everywhere after molting."

I wasn't sure where Marjorie was going with this, but I'd seen the dried husks of the alien-looking insects covering the tree trunks and littering the grass. I nodded.

"Sometimes we have to do that too—grow out of our old skins."

I still didn't know what to say and, for some reason, couldn't bring myself to look Marjorie in the eye. She didn't need me to say anything. She tucked a piece of hair that had escaped my ponytail behind my ear, smiled softly, and walked out through the screen door, letting it close silently behind her.

I stood in the hall of the Mansion for a few minutes, alone. Finally I walked back out to the Bowl, taking my seat beside Pookie and Ruby.

"You okay?" Pookie asked, probably wondering why I'd been gone so long.

Ruby climbed back into my lap, and I nodded. The drone of the cicadas that normally blended seamlessly into the camp's background noise now buzzed in my ears. The special kind of cicada that Marjorie had mentioned, a cousin to the ones chirping now, burrowed in the ground and only emerged every seventeen years. When they did, it was a big deal, reported in all the local papers and on television. I was seventeen. How much longer, I wondered, until I could shed this skin that suddenly felt so small.

I had to see Ransome that night. Since he'd been COD Sunday, and I'd been on duty last night, I'd only caught glimpses of him out on the lake, when he'd wave as his boat passed the swim dock, and my heart would stand still. If I could just talk with him, I told myself, everything would be okay. He'd make it okay.

After Taps, I rushed through a painfully long chapter of *Harry Potter*, grabbed my fleece, and hurried to the riflery range. When I got there, I kept walking. I continued on the path the boys took from the range to Brownstone. I hoped, if I had timed it right, that I might meet Ransome on the way and casually suggest we skip the riflery range and hang out somewhere else, just the two of us. I couldn't deal with Winn that night, especially not after my fight with Katie Bell. Her words had been gnawing at the pit of my stomach since we parted in the Yard: "If ditching your best friend is grown-up, then I don't mind being a kid."

I was smart or lucky, because as I walked slowly along the pitch-black path, wondering whether this was such a good idea after all, I heard voices getting closer and footsteps. It was Brownies.

The one in front stopped suddenly and swung his flashlight in my direction. "Helena!" a voice exclaimed. "You scared the crap out of me."

I squinted against the bright light in my eyes. "Sorry, Buzz."

I smiled awkwardly as the guys filed past me. All but

Ransome, who stopped. His hands, like they often were, were shoved deep in the pockets of his Carhartts.

"You sneaking into Brownstone for a panty raid or something?" Just from his voice, I could tell his eyes were crinkling at the corners, the way they did when he smiled.

I wanted to wrap my arms around his waist, but the other guys weren't out of sight yet.

"No." I laughed. "I just thought I'd cut you off at the pass." I hesitated and then thought of the misery of sharing the riflery range with Ransome and Winn, and continued, "How do you feel about going somewhere else tonight—just us? I've had kind of a bad day. . . ."

I was underplaying it, with Katie Bell's words still burning in my chest.

Ransome grinned and did what I had wanted him to do, setting his hands on my hips and pulling me in toward him.

"You want to go to the archery range?" he asked. "I can run back and get a blanket."

"No, that's okay," I answered, maybe too quickly. "We can sit on the ground. I can put my fleece down."

I didn't want Ransome to think I wanted to have sex again. I just needed to talk, to be near him.

"Are you sure?" he asked, pulling my hips in closer.

I pushed him away playfully. "Yes." I grinned. "I'm sure."

"Okay," he said easily, catching my drift.

I held his hand as he led me down the trail. It forked to the left and ended at a clearing that was Brownstone's archery range. Under the moon I could make out four large, round hay bales, each affixed with a giant multicolored target.

"So I guess Beverly's no longer the star of target practice," I observed.

"I wish I could say my better judgment won out, but Dad found them when he came to mow the grass. Made me take them down. Is this okay?" he asked, looking around and at me.

I nodded and sat Indian-style on the ground. Sharp grass poked at my butt. I started to remove my fleece to sit on, but Ransome stopped me.

"You'll be cold," he said, and pulled his own jacket over his head, laying it down instead.

"Now *you'll* be cold."

"That's all right. You can keep me warm," he joked in an intentionally cheesy voice, as he leaned toward me.

We kissed for a while before I pulled away. I licked my lips, which tasted like him, and looked down at my hands in my lap.

"I had a bad day," I repeated quietly. I had hoped

after my first mention of it on the path that Ransome would ask what happened.

"What's up?"

Ransome propped his weight on his hands behind him. His outstretched legs were long, at least six inches longer than mine, and for once my size-nine-and-a-half hiking boots looked almost small in comparison.

I nervously dug a tooth into my lower lip, then proceeded to tell him about Winn and Katie Bell, how they'd both confronted me and were now pissed. Really pissed.

"I'm sorry, Hel," he said when I had finished. "That sucks."

I waited for him to say more, but that was all he offered.

That's it? I thought, mildly ticked off. I'd just spilled my guts, telling him how, in the last twenty-four hours, two of my closest friends had both bitched me out, accused me of being a bad friend and person, and possibly disowned me, and "that sucks" was all he had to say about it?

"I know it sucks," I said, annoyed. I'd been waiting all day and all night to be here with him, but suddenly it didn't hold the comfort I thought it would. "Is that all you're gonna say?"

"What do you want me to say?" His voice was tinged with irritation now too. "They had no right to get mad at you. That sucks. Forget about them."

"I can't forget about them, Ransome. They're my friends . . . or they *were* my friends." I mumbled the last part mostly to myself.

"They don't sound like friends I'd want."

I looked at him in disbelief, then turned away. "Well, it's complicated," I said angrily.

"Sounds like it. . . ."

Neither of us spoke for what was probably only a few strained moments but felt like forever. This was not at all how I'd pictured this going. I'd imagined lying in Ransome's arms, confessing my soul and unburdening my troubles. Not bickering.

"I'm sorry," I said, finally buckling. "I didn't mean to get mad at you. I'm just upset, that's all."

"I know." He hugged his arm around my shoulders tightly. "Come here."

He pulled me to him, kissing me and eventually leaning back so that I was on top of him. After a while, his hand drifted to my zipper. I fought with whether to stop him or not. It felt good, but something else had been bothering me as well.

"Ransome," I said as he fumbled with the button at the top of my jeans. "I need to ask you something."

He stopped. "Okay," he said tentatively.

I leaned against his chest. "The other night . . . you had a condom with you. . . ." It was hard for me to say the words. They felt foreign and embarrassing, like the words you were forced to say in health class. They *were* words you were forced to say in health class. "Were you planning . . . expecting to sleep with me that night?"

Ransome sat up suddenly. "What? No! What kind of guy do you think I am?" He sounded genuinely hurt.

"No," I protested, scared that I had upset him, "it's not that. I just wondered because you seemed . . . prepared."

"Well, yeah." He shrugged like it was the most obvious thing in the world. "Guys carry condoms to be prepared."

"I know," I said quietly, wishing again I hadn't brought it up.

"Look, Hel." His voice was gentle. He lifted my chin, which I still couldn't bring myself to raise so that I was looking him in the eyes. "We don't have to do it again if you don't want to. I wasn't trying to trick you into it or anything. I thought you wanted to."

"I know," I repeated, my concern dissipating in the sincerity in his voice. "I know you wouldn't do that. I don't know why I said anything. I was just thinking about it the other day. . . . I don't want you to think I'm the kind of girl who—"

He stopped me before I could say it. "I know you're not that kind of girl, Hel. That's one of the reasons I like you." He made sure I was looking in his eyes as he said it, so that I could believe him.

"What are the other ones?"

"Do you want a list?"

"Yes." I smiled. "But we only have an hour."

Ransome laughed. "All right then, reason one . . ."

We didn't have sex again. We just kissed until I settled into the familiar crook between his shoulder and his chest. Before long, Ransome was breathing so steadily I didn't know if he was awake or asleep. I couldn't sleep, partly because I pictured us waking up in the morning with a circle of gaping little boys standing around us, but also because I had a nagging feeling like I was missing something. Like I'd forgotten a *thing*, left my keys or my wallet somewhere—but bigger.

All I'd wanted tonight, what I was asking for, was some understanding, someone to listen and nod and say, "I'm sorry," and mean it. Someone not to try to fix things, or tell me to blow it off, or gloss over it; just someone to say, "I know what you mean."

Lying there, I realized all I wanted was a girlfriend. Because for the first time in my life, surrounded by my Southpoint sisters, I couldn't find one. How had things gotten so complicated, I wondered, at the most uncomplicated place on earth?

Chapter 14

It was Trip Day, and I'd been assigned to the creek walk with the littlest girls, who were too young for the sailing trip to the far end of the lake, and not yet interested in hiking one of the nearby mountains because Brownstone boys would be there. Instead we trudged through water that resembled chocolate milk in the creek that snaked through camp. It filled our shorts and weighed down our tennis shoes. The girls didn't know it, but the waste of farm animals in the area, including our own horses, filtered down into the creek every time it rained. Essentially, we were wading waist-high in horse shit. Considering my current frame of mind, that felt about right.

My fights with Katie Bell and Winn, and my frustration with Ransome's inability to make me feel better, had created a gloom like a cloud around me, totally unbefitting of camp. It descended in the mornings and didn't lift until sleep. An undeniable guilt had started to seep in as well. I hadn't meant to turn Winn on Katie Bell. And while I would stubbornly maintain that it wasn't my fault I was a counselor and Katie Bell wasn't, a sinking feeling told me she was at least partially right. I hadn't been a good friend the last couple of weeks. I had left Katie Bell behind.

Katie Bell was my best friend, and that's not the kind of thing that changes just because one of you still counts team games as the highlight of her day, and giggles at boys at the dance. These were things campers were supposed to enjoy—things I'd enjoyed just a year ago, until things became so complicated. Part of me envied Katie Bell. Why hadn't I begged Fred to be a camper one more year with her, instead of Katie Bell begging to be a counselor?

The result of my pushing ahead? Wading behind twelve eight- and nine-year-old girls who still got immeasurable pleasure out of splashing in a muddy creek, while all I could think about was whether the cow pee would turn my tennis shoes yellow.

After a scalding shower before the hiking trip got back and used all the hot water, I felt better, but only on the outside. I decided to kill the time before dinner by finishing my summer reading. At the start of camp I'd barely made a dent in our required reading for AP English, but in the few days since Winn and Katie Bell had stopped talking to me, I'd managed to finish two books and start a third. What had murdered my camp social life was working wonders for my academics.

By the time Soupy blew for dinner, I had just one chapter of *A Separate Peace* left. It was an easy read. I pitied and envied poor Phineas, whose name I loved and who'd done nothing wrong but love life and be a good friend. Sickeningly, though, I felt more like Gene, the narrator, a character too old and jaded for his age. He took his friendships for granted. I cried when Phinny died, and hated Gene. I wouldn't be Gene, I decided as I walked alone down the path to the Mess.

I urged my campers to eat their broccoli as I pushed my own around the plate, and let Pookie at the other end of the table decide who would stack and clear the plates. She initiated a stacking game called Viking, in which the campers had to pretend to row to one side and then the other, until someone messed up and was singled out for duty. I forced a smile as we played, but it wasn't real.

After dinner I lingered, wiping down my table extra slow, and even getting the broom out to sweep under and around it. When there was nothing more to clean, I wandered out of the Mess, careful not to let the screen door slam behind me. As I left I noticed the Spirit Award plaque nailed above the door. The green letters of Winn's name leaped out at me. I wondered who would get the award this year and hoped it would be Katie Bell.

Outside, girls were milling around and waiting for Evening Gathering. With nothing to do, I figured I'd check our cabin's mailbox again. I'd already checked at rest hour, but maybe I'd missed something.

In the cramped, dusty mailroom that was really an old pantry, I ran my hand inside the cubby labeled "Cabin Nine." Nothing. No letter from my dad, who never wrote anyway, or from my friends at home, who'd forgotten how to handwrite and had been appalled that e-mail and cell phones were banned at camp. Not even a postcard from my mom, who had used my five-week absence as the perfect excuse for a life-enhancing-mind-rejuvenating-relaxation-reflexology-aromatherapy-hatha-vinyasa yoga retreat at some fancy spa in Arizona.

Disappointed, I drifted out of the mailroom empty-handed. Voices floated through the open door of the Oak Room next door. The Oak Room was a rec room on the first floor of the Mansion that was reserved only for cubbies. It was their one official privilege and their unofficial clubhouse. Every year, each cubby carved her initials into the wall, leaving a record of a generation's summer etched indelibly on the Mansion. The summer before, Katie Bell and I had signed next to each other—her initials in big bold bubble letters, and mine in straight neat block letters, followed by the words "Hels Bells." I wondered if she'd sign again this year and, if so, who she'd sign next to.

The overhead lights were off, but a bluish glow lit the faces of the girls seated around the Oak Room's ancient television. It got no reception but still played VHS tapes. The girls were laughing and talking over one another, so they didn't notice when I slid into the back of the room and sat in a folding chair against the wall.

They were watching an old camp video. Judging from the ages of the girls I recognized on the screen, it was from six or seven summers ago. There were Pookie and Megan limping through the three-legged race at Field Day, and Lila spinning at Dizzy Bat before tumbling over like a sloppy drunk. There were young Molly and Amanda, their first year as campers, dressed up as Tweedledee and Tweedledum on Skit Night. As they watched themselves now, they nearly fell off the couch laughing.

And there was Winn, clapping along as she sang camp songs, and Caroline, not as the counselor I felt like she'd always been, but as a cubby. And Sally

McDougal, my counselor my first year at Southpoint, and Sarah and Lizbeth and Marge and Jessie and Lassiter and Mary Price and Mary Katherine . . . so many faces and names. The memories flooded over me. They were too much to catch, like grabbing at water.

Then an image filled the screen that made me suck in a sharp breath. Katie Bell and I stood, dirt smeared across our faces and mouths dyed bright red from Kool-Aid, with our arms slung easily over each other's scrawny shoulders. We were the same height then; puberty was still years off. Our hair was in pigtails, tied with green-and-white ribbons, and we were yelling excitedly over each other, fighting for the camera's attention. Katie Bell had a gap where her front left tooth should have been. I remembered how she'd hated that gap, but loved poking her tongue through it.

"What do you call each other?" the voice behind the camcorder asked, some older counselor now long gone.

On the screen, young Katie Bell and I hollered in unison, "Hels Bells!"

"What was that?" The voice egged us on. "I can't hear you."

Katie Bell and I scrunched our eyes closed and yelled again, louder this time, as the camera focused in close on our cherry red mouths. "Hels Bells!"

The camerawoman laughed, and in the back of the Oak Room, I sobbed. The tears fell hot and fast, streaking my flushed cheeks. I buried my face in my hands to try to muffle the sound, but the girls sitting on the couches in front of me heard anyway and turned, startled to find me in the back of the room. My shoulders heaved up and down, but I couldn't stop.

"Helena?" one of the girls asked.

I looked up, wiping at my cheeks. I was ashamed to have trespassed on their privacy, ashamed to be crying, ashamed to be a counselor while they were still campers.

"Are you okay?" Amanda asked, alarmed.

I nodded, trying to stop my runny nose with the back of my hand. "Yeah. Sorry."

I raised pleading eyes to meet Katie Bell's. She was looking at me, perplexed but unmoved.

"Can we talk?" My voice struggled from my choked throat.

Without a word, Katie Bell stood up from the couch and started to walk out of the room. I watched, terrified that she was leaving for good; there would be no mending of friendships here. But when she reached the door, Katie Bell turned to look back, and I understood that she was saying yes.

Leaving the other girls to exchange worried glances,

I followed Katie Bell out of the Oak Room.

"Softball diamond?" she asked.

I nodded. On the Yard, campers and counselors were hanging out under the oak trees. I didn't want to make a scene. Turning my tear-stained face from them, I walked silently beside Katie Bell past the Mansion, over the footbridge that crossed the creek I'd waded in that afternoon, past the cabins, and up toward the softball diamond.

From its location on top of a small hill that sloped gently down to the lake, the softball diamond offered a glimpse of the water. When we sat on the bleachers, Katie Bell and I both stared out at the sparkle of the low sun on the glassy surface.

At first neither of us said a word as I tried to stop crying, swallowing down the great hiccups of tears that kept coming. When they finally subsided, I turned toward Katie Bell. Still, I couldn't look her in the eyes, so I stared down at the grainy red dirt of the softball diamond. This was where Katie Bell and I used to search for Indian arrowheads before it had become our place to talk.

"I'm sorry." The weight of the small words surprised me as they tumbled into my lap.

Katie Bell's feet crossed and uncrossed. "I know," she said.

I waited for more, but when she fell quiet again, I continued. "Everything's different." I struggled to find words. "Camp's different. It's not camp anymore. It's like . . . the real world, just like the rest of our lives." I stopped, unhappy with how poorly I was expressing myself.

Katie Bell drew in a long breath but still didn't speak.

"I never thought it would be like this," I said. "Not here. There aren't supposed to be cliques and rumors and guy drama at Southpoint."

"Maybe not for the kids . . ." Katie Bell faded off.

But I wasn't a kid anymore, she implied. I'd crossed the line and was now looking back from the other side, wondering how I'd gotten here. But how was I supposed to know it would be like this? Like one day you're a kid, and the next you're . . . not? I thought growing up was a process, something you did over years, not a summer.

There was a sickening dread ballooning inside of me. "Oh God, Katie Bell," I said. I felt like I might cry again.

Finally I looked into her gray eyes. Katie Bell's face was thinner than I remembered. She'd lost some weight at camp. Instead of her usual ponytail, her red hair fell down around her shoulders, and even though the sun had brought out her freckles, especially across her nose, they didn't have the usual effect of making her look younger. They were pretty—that quirky beauty you see in models and foreign actresses.

I searched there for an answer, praying Katie Bell had a rope to tow me back. Her face softened.

"I mean, you're only seventeen, Hel!" She laughed lightly, and her eyes widened. "It's not like life's over . . . but you *are* seventeen."

I nodded. In a year I'd be going away to college. There would be freedom, independence, new relationships, bigger adventures. That's what they told you. And that's what I wanted, right? That's what I had been looking forward to for so long. So why did it feel like I was losing something in the bargain?

"I'll be seventeen in a few months too, ya know," Katie Bell reminded me.

"I know," I replied softly. "I think maybe that's what's been bothering me. You get this last summer and I don't. I guess I'm a little jealous. You get to do whatever you want for activities, and I have to stay at the swim dock with bitchy Winn and Sarah. And you get to do things like the scavenger hunt and tubing and stuff . . ." I faded off.

It wasn't really about the things Katie Bell still got to do as a camper; it was how she felt doing it. That's what I missed. I wanted *that* back.

"Yeah." Katie Bell gave a reluctant one-shouldered shrug and nodded. "It's fun. But it can't be like that forever, Hel," she said gently.

"I know." I picked at the dirt under my fingernails. "Sometimes I just wish we could go back."

I lifted my head, and both of us stared out at the slice of lake visible over the pine trees. Something glinted on the water, a boat making its way back to Brownstone. Its shiny fiberglass caught the sunlight and reflected it over all that distance to us.

"Me too," said Katie Bell unexpectedly, after I thought the conversation had been dropped. "Sometimes I wish we could go back too."

That was the last either of us spoke, although we stayed at the softball diamond until the chill in the air gave us goose bumps, and we were forced to go to our cabins for sweatshirts before Evening Gathering. But while nothing was spoken, everything was said. For the first time that summer, Katie Bell and I stood on the same side of the line, which was on neither side. We didn't know where we belonged. Everything felt like we were giving up something we weren't ready to let go of just yet.

Chapter 15

It hadn't been easy, halfway through camp, to get reassigned from the swim dock to the boat dock. Nan, in charge of scheduling as the oldest counselor, had raised a quizzical eyebrow, wondering why I wanted to give up my coveted spot on the lifeguard stand. Besides, I'd never been all that good at sailing as a camper.

It was a stretch, I knew, but I told Nan that Pookie, Caroline, and Lizbeth looked like they needed the help, and Winn and Sarah didn't mind. In fact, I'd mentioned to both of them the day before that I thought they had everything under control at the swim dock. If not, I was sure someone else would be happy to take my place. Winn had looked at me for a second longer than was natural. Her lips parted, as if she might say something, might finally own up to what had happened between us over the past week. But then she reconsidered and nodded in agreement, turning to climb up the lifeguard ladder.

Nan erased my name from the swimming block on the large whiteboard where she worked out the day's activity schedule and Sharpied me in under "boating." "I'll pull Lila from crafts," she said to herself.

I thanked her with a sigh of relief, wondering if she knew my real reason for wanting to switch. It didn't matter.

Hopefully, the boat dock would offer some relief from the drama. In addition (and, admittedly, not the last thing I'd considered when requesting the reassignment), it meant I'd get to see Ransome during the day. He and Buzz often brought the motorboats over from Brownstone. Just those few seconds—his smile, an inside joke, a secret wink—would keep me going until I could see him next.

I still hadn't told anyone what had happened in the hayloft, not even Katie Bell. I wasn't ready to say it out loud. Still, all I could think about lately was how Ransome and I could be together after camp ended. It consumed my thoughts through rest hour, meals, while Winn and Sarah were ignoring me on the dock.

I'd never been in love before. Maybe this was it, I thought. This crazy need just to be near him that didn't fade even when I was with him—it certainly felt like love. It sounded like love.

But there was still that teeny, tiny, dust particle–size part of me that wondered if I just *wanted* it to be love. I couldn't imagine not dating—real-world dating, not camp dating—the guy I'd lost my virginity to. When that possibility came barging into my daydreamy thoughts, I shoved it away. Because what would that mean about me? That wasn't the Helena who'd come to camp, and I didn't want it to be the Helena who left.

I didn't want to think about it, but the truth was— once the kids were gone, and the cabins were locked, and it was time to return to real life, where Ransome was in college in Knoxville and I was in Nashville—I didn't know what would happen. So I ignored the end of camp and looked at the boat dock as an opportunity, where maybe just glances between us could bring Ransome and me closer, could build a real relationship. One that lasted beyond the daydreams of camp.

When I reported to the waterfront a few minutes late because I'd had to mop up a milk spill at my table after breakfast, Lizbeth was already standing at the end of one of the long docks that jutted out into the lake. Her hands were on her thin hips. Although I couldn't see her eyes under her green Southpoint visor, I got the impression she was counting the dozen or so Sunfish, Lasers, and Flying Scotts bobbing in the water. I wasn't sure if she had seen me, but surely she'd heard my footsteps on the wooden planks. She didn't turn.

"Hey," I said.

Lizbeth finished counting before she looked up. "Hey," she answered.

I wondered what Winn had told her, and wished Pookie had been the one to meet me on the dock.

"What can I do to help?" The water lapped peacefully against the sides of the boats.

"Well..." Lizbeth sighed, as the door of the boathouse creaked behind me and Pookie and Caroline walked up to deliver two armloads of orange life preservers. They dumped them in a pile on the dock between us.

"Hey, Hel." Pookie smiled. At least she was happy to see me.

"We have the Catfish and Carps for first and second activities," Lizbeth continued. "If you stay on the dock as the safety counselor, the three of us can go out with the girls who want instruction. Third period, the Minnows have tubing. The guys will come to pick them up."

"Maybe you could get their ski vests on while we tie up the sailboats?" offered Caroline. "It's kind of hectic when we have tubing or skiing right after sailing."

Tubing was always a favorite activity. Kind of funny, as all it really involved was holding on for dear life to an inflatable rubber disk dragged at breakneck speed behind a motorboat. Wiping out, which often included a face full of water and an atomic wedgie, was part of the fun.

"Sounds like a plan," I said.

With the other counselors out on the water, things were quiet on the dock. Lookouts never had much to do but think. I let my mind drift listlessly.

Of course my first thought was whether Ransome would be the one to take the Minnows tubing. I carefully watched the motorboats pulling Brownstone campers behind them, but from this distance, I couldn't make out who was driving.

By the time the bugle blew for third activity period, my anticipation was killing me. Ruby and the other Minnows were skipping down the hill toward the boat dock, picking up speed.

"Slow down!" Lizbeth called, hunched over a Sun-fish she was tying down. She straightened and turned to me, squinting under her visor. "Helena, will you get them checked in and into their ski vests? The boat should be here soon."

As if on cue, the roar of an approaching engine

drowned out the excited chattering of the Minnows. It slowed to a steady chug as Buzz steered the boat toward the dock. Ransome was next to him. Behind his sunglasses I couldn't see his eyes, but I could see his smile.

"What are you doing down here?" he asked as he tossed two coiled ropes onto the dock. They landed with two loud thuds, as he jumped nimbly off the boat and onto the dock to help me tie it down.

I gave him a flirtatious smile as I figure-eighted the bow line around one of the large metal cleats. "They needed more help," I half lied.

"I got it," Lizbeth said impatiently, coming around behind me to unwrap and retie the knot I'd just made. "Can you just get the girls in their life vests?"

I blushed. "Sure."

Ransome winked at me as I turned, and my blush deepened.

"All right," I called, smiling inside. The girls rushed to form a line on the dock in front of me. "Everyone grab a vest, and I'll make sure you're all strapped in correctly."

They scurried for the blue neoprene mountain of ski vests, picking through the pile for the newest, least moldy ones.

"One at a time!" I shouted over their squeals. But outside of the flurry, I noticed Ruby hanging back.

"Ruby," I called. "What's wrong?"

"Nothing."

"Aren't you excited to go tubing?"

She shrugged and nodded.

I commanded a squirming Minnow to hold still as I snapped the plastic clasps of her preserver. "Is this your first time on the motorboat, Ruby?"

Again she nodded slowly.

"Okay. Don't worry. It'll be so much fun you won't want to stop! I promise." I waved Ruby to me and knelt down to help her untwist the straps of a vest.

"There." I smiled when she was all secure. She gave me a weak smile back.

As the first girls piled on, Lizbeth and I tossed the towlines into the boat. Buzz shifted the engine into gear, and the boat chugged away from the dock, picking up speed as it got farther from the shore. Ransome looked back once, and I smiled and waved.

"Have fun!" I shouted after them.

Ruby was in the last group to go out in the boat. Like a good friend, Melanie had waited with her, cross-examining each returning group. "See?" she would say eagerly to Ruby. Still, their thrilled testimonials weren't convincing enough for Ruby. She stood tight-lipped and serious in her life vest, her arms wrapped protectively around her, and when the time finally came to climb aboard, she wouldn't give Ransome her hand to help her on.

"Have you ever been tubing before?" Ransome asked.

Ruby's curls shook side to side.

"Would you feel better if Helena came with us?" He turned his green-flecked eyes on me. I melted, watching him be so cute with Ruby.

Ruby nodded her head and looked to me eagerly.

"Is that okay?" I asked Lizbeth, beside me.

"Sure." She shrugged and glanced at the diving watch on her wrist. "Y'all just have to be quick. The bugle's gonna blow in fifteen minutes."

"No problem," I said, and climbed quickly into the boat after Ruby.

A camper named Jillian from Cabin One East volunteered to tube first. She squealed when she jumped from the boat into the cold water. Ransome explained to her how to lie on her belly across the large inner tube and hold on, with elbows bent, to the tow rope at the front. She was to give a thumbs-up for more speed and a thumbs-down to go slower. Jillian nodded and doggie-paddled to the tube bobbing behind the boat.

As we coasted around the lake, Ruby and Melanie giggled in the bow, their hair whipping behind them in the wind. Ransome sat with me in the stern. I kept an eye on Jillian to make sure she was okay as we picked up speed—she bumped over the wake, grinning and squinting comically against the spray in her face—but my attention was on Ransome.

He was facing into the wind, and it tousled even his short hair. It was the golden down, though, on the tan arm lying on the seat cushion next to mine, that I couldn't stop staring at. And the large callused hands, which I still couldn't believe had wandered over my body. Suddenly I had the uncontrollable urge to touch him, just his hand even, just to make contact.

Fighting the urge, I turned my attention to Jillian. Finally her hands were tiring. She let go of the tow rope and drifted in the wake while Buzz made a careful, wide arc and circled around to pick her up. As she climbed out of the water, jubilant and shivering from cold and excitement, Melanie plunged in for her turn.

From the helm, Buzz called over the low hum of the engine, "Hel, have you ever driven one of these?"

"A Whaler? No, I've only sailed," I yelled.

"Wanna give it a try?"

My eyebrows arched. "You mean drive the boat?"

"It's not hard," said Buzz. "Ransome can show you."

"Yeah," Ransome said, moving to the wheel. "Come on." He cocked his head with a sly smile.

Melanie had already heaved herself onto the tube

and was floating expectantly behind the boat.

"Okay . . ." I said. There was no way to say no to that smile.

Buzz moved back to the stern and reclined across the seat, shouting instructions to Melanie. I stood at the wheel, and Ransome stood very close behind me. With one hand on the steering wheel and the other on the throttle, I figured it couldn't be so different from driving a car.

Ransome wrapped his hand over mine. He clicked the unlock button on the throttle and gently pushed the lever, and we idled forward. Slowly he continued pushing the throttle until the boat accelerated, raising the bow in front and churning a white wake behind us. I nervously glanced over his shoulder to make sure Melanie was okay. She was happily bouncing along and giving the thumbs-up. I laughed and smiled at Ransome, my hair whipping into my eyes and mouth.

"She wants to go faster," I said, but the wind stole my words, and Ransome leaned closer for me to say it again. My lips brushed against his ear, and again I had an urge to kiss it. Not possible, not here. "She wants to go faster," I repeated, feeling slightly dizzy from the rush of hormones and the movement of the boat.

Ransome nodded, pushed the throttle forward more, and stepped back to let me steer.

It was a powerful feeling, being both in control and a little out of it. The water blurred under us. The lake had never felt so big before. From the dock the lake seemed constant, definable, but from the speeding boat, it rushed by, expanding and contracting with every tiny rotation of the wheel. The slightest redirection and a new perspective instantly unfolded. I understood why the guys were drawn to motorboating more than the sailing the girls loved.

I drove us out to the middle of the lake, then turned back toward the dock in a wide arc, sending Melanie flying over the wake. I corrected, snaking to the other side, and she bumped back over the wake and behind the boat again.

Ruby and Buzz were yelling, but I couldn't hear them because of the wind. "What?" I mouthed to Ruby.

"She wants to do it again," Ransome shouted into my ear. "Melanie wants to go over the wake again."

"Okay." I checked the horizon for other boats. There was one, another motorboat—larger and sleeker than our Boston Whaler, definitely not a camp boat, probably one of the vacationers nearby—but it had already passed safely in front of us. The wake behind it was small, just choppy enough to give Melanie a fun ride without throwing her from the tube, so I turned the wheel to drive over the end of the boat's wake.

"Helena!"

Two hands shot around me from behind and grabbed the steering wheel, yanking it to the right.

As we banked sharply away from the wake of the other boat, the Whaler practically sideways in the water from the sharpness of the turn, I saw it—the towline dragging a water skier behind the other boat. His head was barely visible above the water. We would have hit him.

People always describe accidents as if they happened in slow motion, but there was no deceleration of time for me, no neat splicing of events so that I could see it all in linear progression, like beads on a string. Instead it was as if time collapsed in on itself, like a telescope. I saw the skier at the same moment that the raised bottom of our boat scraped sickeningly against the side of another boat we hadn't seen behind us, and the same moment my head smacked against the surface of the water like a wall, and the same moment lightning seemed to split my head in two, and the same moment the water enveloped me. But the blackness seeped in slowly, like an ink bleed, until I was gone, and all that remained was water.

Chapter 16

Beep. Beep. Beep. Beep. Beep . . .

Chapter 17

The sound was even, steady. At first I thought it was the instruments on the boat. Then maybe my heart. My eyes opened, slits through which I could see out but no one could see in. Only there was no one there, just a wall of machines to my left and right.

The beeps continued in a tinny march through the fog that swaddled my brain. I opened my eyes wider, and pain shot to the back of my skull. The lights in the room were bright, almost blinding. Fluoride? Fluorescent? What was the word?

With great care I rolled my head on the pillow, and my eyes roved over the small room. Beige. A metal chart hung on the back of the door.

My chin dropped to my chest. On the pilled blue cotton bedspread lay a pale slender arm. It surprised me to follow the hand to the forearm to the elbow to the shoulder . . . and realize it was my own. Clear tubes snaked from the—my—bandaged wrist, tethering me to the bed, to the room, to the world.

My brain strained, wanting to lift my other hand to pull the tubes from the veins coursing like thin blue rivers under the skin of my inner wrist. My fingers twitched, but my arm lay there as heavy as lead. My heart seemed to rattle my ribs like a prisoner on iron bars. My breath was coming shorter and faster now. The beeping of the machines didn't reassure me anymore; it jangled my nerves.

Where? Why? The words rose out of a messy, murky mind. The beeps grew faster, frantic. Suddenly an alarm sounded, high-pitched and shrieking. What was happening? Where was I? Why was I alone?

The door swung open, the metal clipboard nearly falling from its hook. A heavyset black woman in pink pajamas trundled toward my bed, yelling to the two women who followed her. She took my tender wrist, feeling for my pulse. Words flew above my head, words I did not recognize, as the nurses—that's what they were? Nurses?—studied the glowing green peaks and valleys on the beeping machines that screamed in the way I wanted to but couldn't find the voice.

The large woman leaned over me, her breasts in my face.

"Where am I?" I tried to ask. "What happened?" But nothing came.

I searched the faces around me for an answer, some sort of reassurance. More people had entered the room now, people with name tags on white coats.

"I'm gonna need an EEG!" one of the white-coated men shouted, lifting my eyelid, then the other. He waved a pen in front of my eyes. "Page Dr. Fiennes," he ordered, speaking in my face but not to me.

"What happened?" I tried again, but it came out as a strangled squawk.

My right leg jerked involuntarily, but my left remained immobile. Then a pressure on my wrist as the nurse inserted a needle into my IV and another nurse massaged the bag swinging from its metal pole.

Reality became as liquid as the clear fluid in the bag. I was sinking as peacefully as a rock to the bottom of a green lake shot through with light. Only I wasn't scared this time. The urgent beeping continued, but it didn't matter. I just wanted to sleep a little more; I wanted to explain to the tense, urgent faces around me, *Don't worry. I'm safe and warm here. Just a little longer . . .*

I didn't know how much time had passed, but when I woke again, the benevolent fuzziness was gone. I hurt all over with a dull, vibrating pain. There was a warm weight on my hand, someone holding it. Carefully I turned my head and saw that the person holding my hand was my mother. Her eyes filled with tears as she reached to brush my hair from my cheek.

"Hi, honey." A tear slipped from her eye and ran down her cheek, leaving a stripe of mascara.

"What happens?" My voice came out strange and thin. I knew I wasn't speaking right. Something was off. My joints ached and my throat felt dry, like tissue paper. My body didn't belong to me.

"Why? Why?" I repeated my question without meaning to. "Why?"

"Shhh." Another inky tear. "Helena," my mother said in a tight, controlled voice, "honey, you were in an accident. At camp. Your boat ran into another one, and you fell overboard. You hit your head."

I remembered now, driving the boat, the panicked moment when we cut away to avoid the skier, the edge of the boat catching me as I fell over the side. . . .

"You am okay?"

My mother flinched. "Yes, honey, you're gonna be okay. You've been . . . asleep for a while. There was some trauma to your head. But the doctors say you're gonna be fine."

I looked around the room. It smelled like beach. Bleach, I corrected in my head. Why were my words getting all confused?

"Ruby," I said suddenly.

My mother knit her brow, trying to understand me, thinking I'd misplaced my words again.

"Ransome. Melanie . . ." I struggled but couldn't remember the other girl's name.

"The other kids in the boat?" My mom finally understood. "They're fine, sweetie. One of the boys, Ransome, broke his leg, and the girls had a few bumps and bruises, but they're fine. You were the only one who sustained . . ." The words were too much for her, and she cut off, crying into her hands.

"Mom," I said, squeezing her hand. At the slight pressure, her mood lightened, and she dabbed at her cheeks with a stained tissue.

"You're gonna be fine too," she repeated, as much to herself as to me. "Fine" was the word of the moment.

"My head hurts."

"I know, sweetie."

"Is Dad here?"

"Yes. He went to get some coffee. Do you want to see him?"

"Not yet."

She nodded.

"I might sleep now."

"Okay." She sounded hesitant. But I had already

closed my eyes and was drifting back to the warm, dark place.

I was dreaming of camp. It was so vivid, more real than any dream I'd ever had. Every detail, every smell and sight and sound and taste . . . But someone was insistently saying my name.

"Helena . . . Helena . . . you have a visitor."

It was dark outside now. The only light in the room came from the lamp beside my bed. The nurse, the one in pink from earlier, only now she was in purple, was standing over me again. She smiled when I opened my eyes.

"Sorry to wake you, baby, but the doctors said it'd be good for you to talk some, and she's been waiting. Visiting hours are almost over."

She stepped back to reveal Katie Bell.

"Hey, Hel."

I smiled. "Hey. Thanks for coming." It felt like the right thing to say.

"Are you kidding?" She swatted away the impossible idea that she might not come, and perched on the side of my bed. "Oh!" she exclaimed, jumping up and looking at the nurse, who was fiddling with a knob on one of my machines. "Is it okay if I sit on her bed?"

"Sure, baby. You've got fifteen minutes before visiting hours are over, but I'll give you twenty." The nurse winked and shuffled out of the room, closing the door quietly behind her.

Katie Bell sat awkwardly again on the side of the bed.

"It's okay," I said. "You can really sit. It doesn't hurt."

She pushed herself back. "How are you?"

I'd never been so glad to see her. After all the drama, maybe we'd be okay. I sighed, not too deeply, as it hurt my head. "Fine—or that's what my mom keeps telling me." I forced a smile.

"Good."

"I bet everyone at camp's freaking out, huh? Is Fred pissed?"

Katie Bell gave me a strange look. She tried to hide it quickly, but I'd already seen it.

"What?" I asked.

"Hel . . ." she said softly, in a very un-Katie-Bell-like voice.

"What? Katie Bell, you're scaring me. Did something happen to Ruby or Ransome or—"

"No, no," she said quickly. "That's not it. It's just . . . Camp's over, Helena. It ended three weeks ago."

I looked at her, confused, not fully grasping what she was trying to tell me.

Her expression changed from one of confusion to one of sympathy. "Hel," she said, "you've been in a coma for almost five weeks."

Chapter 18

"Five weeks?" I asked.

Katie Bell nodded slowly. "I thought they told you. I thought . . ."

I blinked and swallowed down a wave of bile trying to force itself from my empty stomach. The vividness of my dreams swept over me again. The smell of hay was suddenly as strong as if there was a bale of it in the hospital room.

"Is . . . is Ransome here?" I asked, changing the subject. I wanted to see him. I wanted him to hold my hand and explain what had happened.

Katie Bell inhaled sharply. "No, Hel. He *was* here, after the accident. Almost every day. But the doctors, they didn't know . . . He had to go back to school."

The same bile rose again in my throat. I squeezed

my eyes shut against the tears. "He went back?"

"Yeah, Hel. He had to, but—"

"Katie Bell . . . I had sex with him." Finally I had told someone.

Surprise cast a momentary shadow over Katie Bell's eyes, but she hid it instantly. "It's okay," she said. She paused, and a crooked smile crept to her mouth. "Was it good?"

"I don't know." I laughed, but it hurt. I tried to remember, but the details of my dreams and my memories were all jumbled. "Yeah, I guess. But . . . he's not here?"

I quickly glanced at the door as if there might have been some mistake, and Ransome was, in fact, waiting for me behind the door with a fistful of purple tulips, even though he couldn't know they were my favorites, because I'd never had the chance to tell him.

Of course he wasn't there, and Katie Bell shook her head gently to confirm this when my eyes returned to her face.

"But there is someone else here to see you," she said hopefully. "Do you think you're up for it?"

I had no idea who it would be—maybe a friend from home? Fred and Marjorie?

"Yeah," I answered, pushing myself up against the pillows. "Who is it?"

"Hang on a sec. . . ."

Katie Bell opened the door and stepped out into the hall. Moments later the door swung open again, and behind Katie Bell stood Winn. She took a tentative step toward my bed. Winn was the last person I expected to see in my hospital room—especially with Katie Bell.

"Hey," she said quietly. "I heard you were up."

I felt Katie Bell watching me for my reaction, maybe to see if I remembered the way things had been with Winn before the accident.

For a second I didn't remember. I only felt the return of a vague clawing anxiety in my stomach. But when she spoke, it all came rushing back—what Katie Bell had told me about Winn and Ransome, questioning Ransome about it in the hayloft, being dragged out to the softball diamond to be interrogated, and then dropped.

Suddenly I felt very tired again. But I didn't want to sleep. I'd been sleeping for five weeks.

Katie Bell must have thought I was wondering how Winn knew I was awake, because she quickly pointed out that Winn had been e-mailing her to check on me.

I nodded and reached for the plastic cup filled with water by my bed, but couldn't reach it. Winn, who was closest, jumped to put it in my hand.

"Thanks," I murmured.

Something in Winn's pale blue eyes said she wanted to tell me something very badly, but she didn't know how. It made me nervous and unsure of how to act. I accidentally dropped the cup, and it went clattering across the linoleum floor. The sound was startling in the quiet of the hospital. My grip still wasn't strong, and my clumsiness embarrassed me.

Both girls sprang to the floor. Katie Bell replaced the cup on my bedside table as Winn mopped uselessly at the water with a couple of napkins left over from a lunch of broth and Jell-O. I was starving, but my stomach was queasy from the medications I was on.

"I think I saw a nurse's station down the hall. I'll go get some more napkins," said Katie Bell, avoiding my eyes because she knew they would plead with her not to go.

"Okay," Winn agreed, crouching on the floor. She stood, wadding the soaked napkins in her hands, and went to throw them in the wastebasket in the corner of the room.

There was something about Winn's appearance that was throwing me off. At first I attributed it to my condition and the general feeling I had about everything around me, like when a word was on the tip of your tongue—but the *world* was on the tip of my tongue.

Then I realized what it was. Winn was dressed in fall clothes, not the normal summer stuff I was used to seeing her in. The bathing suit had been replaced by jeans and a short-sleeve, button-up shirt. Instead of flip-flops, Winn wore red flats, and weirdest of all, she was wearing jewelry: large pearl earrings and a gold signet ring on her right hand. She saw me looking at it, and instinctively, her hand moved to cover it.

"It's my school ring," she explained, almost apologetically.

I nodded, realizing that if as much time had passed as Katie Bell said, my friends at home were probably receiving theirs any day now.

Winn and I looked at each other without a word passing between us until it was obvious Katie Bell was not coming back with paper towels just yet. The clock ticked on the wall behind me, each tock more awkward than the last.

Finally Winn sat in one of the mauve pleather chairs at the foot of my bed. "Helena, I'm sorry."

It's only because you feel guilty, I thought. Because I might not have been on that boat if I'd still felt welcome on the swim dock.

"And it's not because I feel guilty," Winn continued, making me wonder if one of the side effects of head trauma was the ability of others to suddenly read your mind. "I was sorry before the accident. I just didn't know how to say it."

"Why?" I asked, relieved I could speak again without involuntarily repeating myself or using the wrong words.

"Maybe I was just being proud or stubborn. I don't know. . . ."

"No. I meant, why are you sorry? Why did you ditch

me? I thought we were friends, and then suddenly you
. . . turned on me." I couldn't control the betrayal and
hurt in my voice.

Winn's eyes glistened. Tears were a familiar sight in
my room these days. Only, strangely, I was the only one
not shedding them. Still not a tear since I'd woken up, as
if my tear ducts had been injured in the accident as well.

"We *were* friends. I mean, we *are* . . . I hope we are."
Winn's voice quavered. She held her elbows tightly, as
if looking for something to hold on to and finding only
herself.

"Part of me was embarrassed and jealous about
Ransome, I guess. He chose you. I had liked him and he'd
barely even noticed me, and then you came along. . . . But
it was more than that too." Winn considered her words
as she said them. "I kind of felt like your older sister, ya
know? I was looking out for you, and you looked up to me
. . . or, I felt like you did. Then all of a sudden, it was like
you could see through me, and I wasn't your older sister
anymore. I was just some jealous girl. I felt stupid."

It was the completely wrong reaction, I knew even as
it happened (they had told me my emotions might be out
of whack), but I laughed. It started as a silent chuckle.
Then it grew until I was shaking in the bed, and there
were finally tears running down my face. Winn looked
startled, unsure of what to do, afraid I was suffering

some kind of breakdown, but as the laughter rose and overtook me, she also started.

"Why are we laughing?" she finally gasped, wiping at her cheeks.

"I don't know," I said, giving up and shrugging as I smiled. "I don't know." I meant to say it twice this time. "You wanted me to look up to you, and all I wanted was for you to think I was cool and not some annoying kid who always followed you around."

As I said it, Katie Bell appeared in the door with a roll of brown paper towels. She stopped when she saw us crying and laughing at the same time. I turned to her, remembering our conversation on the softball diamond. "We all just wanted to be grown-up, but now . . . we are and . . ."

Katie Bell's gray eyes held mine as the reality crashed in on me. I had had my last Southpoint summer. The door had closed on that part of my life as the water had closed over me.

Suddenly I was crying real tears—hot, salty, broken tears. "It's over," I sobbed. "I can't go back."

"Yes, you can," soothed Winn. "You can go back next summer."

"No," I insisted, "it's over." She didn't understand what I meant. The Southpoint I was crying for was gone for me forever.

As I buried my wet face in my hands, I felt four arms twine around me. Katie Bell and Winn sat on either side of me on the hospital bed. They enveloped me.

Winn's chin rested on my bent head. "It's not over Lumberjack," she said.

"It's not, Hel," said Katie Bell.

They held me and rocked me like a little girl until I fell asleep, and I let them.

I dreamed of camp again, more vivid even than the last time. I was in the cabin at night listening to the frogs, then suddenly at the barn—no, on the dock.

When I woke up, I was thirsty, so thirsty my throat felt scratchy and tight, like someone had filled it with sand in my sleep. I turned to my bedside table for the cup of water the nurses kept there. Beside it was the pen and notepad my mother had brought to leave me notes when I fell asleep and she slipped out for coffee or the vending machines. Next to the notepad was something that hadn't been there before: a photograph. I picked it up and studied it.

The photo was of Ruby and Melanie on the last day of camp, at closing ceremonies. Ruby's left arm was in a sling that had been signed in every color of Magic Marker imaginable. Between them, the girls proudly held the plaque bearing the name of the latest winner of the Spirit Award. At first I assumed they had broken tradition and given the girls the award in recognition of the ordeal they'd been through, but then I looked closer. Painted in alternating letters of green and white, next to the year, was stenciled my name.

Two voices in the hallway grew louder until they were outside my room. I quickly wiped the tears from my eyes. It was Katie Bell and Winn.

"I thought you'd left," I said. Their bags were gone, so I'd assumed they went home.

"Nah," answered Katie Bell. "You can't get rid of us that easily."

Winn smiled. "We just went to get you something."

From behind her back, Katie Bell produced a lime green, ice-cold can of Sun-Drop.

"I asked your doctor if you could have caffeine," she said, handing the can to me. "The cute young one. Just don't tell anyone where you got it, 'cause I had to give him a back rub for it." She gave a mischievous shrug of her eyebrows and laughed.

Gratefully, I popped the top of the can and tilted the sweet liquid sunshine to my lips. And for a second, with my eyes closed, I was back at Southpoint, on the cabin porch with Katie Bell, ten again.

EPILOGUE

Reveille

There was a lot of catching up to do when I was released from the hospital. My emotions were haywire and my thoughts disorganized, and while I was lucky my language had returned, there were some cognitive setbacks. At school I wasn't exactly held back, but between rehab, doctor's visits, and the work I'd missed while recovering, it took me two more years to graduate. Katie Bell headed to college a full year before me. I guess that's what they call irony.

When she decided on Belmont University in Nashville, I had to ask, self-consciously, if it was because of me. I was doing fine, I told her. The doctors were amazed. I didn't want to be her charity case.

I wasn't, she scoffed, though she wouldn't deny that being in the same city was a perk. "Hels Bells does Nashvegas!" she'd crowed. I heard her grin over the telephone.

We have a standing coffee date at Bongo Java on Wednesdays and Fridays after school. That will have to end soon, though. I'm heading to college now too, at the University of Tennessee in Knoxville—close enough that I can come home for doctor's appointments, but far enough that my mother can't drive me crazy.

It's a big school, but sometimes I'm afraid I'll see Ransome there, wandering around campus, in the bookstore, at a party. He'll be a senior now. I still picture him, his skin tan and his copper hair lightened by the sun, smiling with his crooked tooth, on the boat dock the day of the accident. Sometimes I want to see him. Sometimes the thought makes me feel as if all the blood is draining from my body.

He called me once, the week I woke up, to see how I was doing. He apologized he couldn't be there. He'd been to the hospital when I was . . . "asleep" (the word everyone preferred to use), but had to get back to school. He hadn't known when I would wake up. He avoided saying "if."

We talked awkwardly for seven minutes exactly. Then he said he had to go but he'd e-mail me. He did and I did, a few times, the period between each correspondence lengthening until finally our communication petered out all together.

Winn and I, on the other hand, have been much

better about keeping in touch. She stayed one more day with me in the hospital, with Katie Bell, and then called once a week to check on my progress and see what was coming back and what was difficult. She said she'd decided, in the hospital, to make her major pre-med.

We talk periodically now, and when we do, our conversations always drift back to camp. She's the only one not afraid to ask me about the accident, the only one who doesn't tiptoe around the subject—even more than the usually blunt Katie Bell. It's a relief and has brought us closer.

It was when I was packing for college, going through the drawers of the desk I rarely use in my bedroom, that I found the journals, the ones the psychologist asked me to keep in the weeks following the coma. Again it was my mother who insisted I see a therapist in addition to my regular doctors, but, unlike the divorce therapists, I liked this one. She didn't ask me to draw pictures with crayons. She asked me to record everything I remembered from that summer in neat, lined notebooks. My dreams too. "Everything" is a lot.

As I wrote, the summer flooded me. Sequences of events were muddy and jumbled at first, tattered memories like dreams, but the sights and sounds and tastes and smells were piercingly clear. Eventually I could remember almost everything leading up to the accident.

It's in the remembering that I've begun to understand. That summer the ground beneath me shifted—slowly and silently, like the continental drifts that created the hills and valleys that cradle Southpoint. The movement was almost imperceptible but for the changing of the landscape.

I do believe part of me died that summer—the part with a Kool-Aid–stained mouth that played tetherball for hours and ate sugar straight from colorful paper tubes. The part that believed childhood was a place that could be returned to every summer. But part of me was born too.

Even though I haven't gone back to camp, am not sure I *could* go back—it would be too different and too hard—I often return to it in my mind. Through the photos and memories and friendships, especially the friendships, Southpoint safely rests in the lap of an internal mountain range, one whose peaks are higher and valleys are lower for my summers there, and that is far more beautiful even than the hills of Tennessee. It's there that I am really home, and my Southpoint sisters are always with me.

Acknowledgments

There are so many people to whom I owe great thanks. First and foremost, my family and friends. I feel very blessed to have them in my life. My editor, Elizabeth Rudnick, who has over the past few years become one of the latter. She is patient and extremely talented. The team at Hyperion for all that goes into the making of a book.

I owe any success in my descriptions of Southpoint to my own time at summer camp. While Southpoint is not intended to be a reflection of that particular camp or a recollection of my or anyone else's experiences, I hope and believe this story is richer for the time I spent there. I am grateful for the camp owners and friends who I've also come to consider family.

I'd like to thank Jessie Yancey for her ideas and feedback; Reid Ward for his insights regarding some of my more subjective medical queries; Nan Stikeleather for her knowledge of boating; and my early readers. Last but never least, I send my love and gratitude to Amma and Appa.

Connecticut Yankee Annie MacRae
has just found out she's heading south
and is going to become . . .

the debutante

kathryn williams

𝒟ℐ𝒮𝒩ℰ𝒴 • HYPERION BOOKS
New York

ONE

A lady doesn't sweat,
she glistens.

The overwhelming scent of magnolia wafted through my bedroom on a humid breeze. If I leaned out the window, I could almost touch the tree's glossy, dark green leaves. When the woman from the real estate company gave us a tour of the house, my mother had optimistically called the tree "charming," but at the moment, in the August heat, the aroma was utterly noxious.

All morning I had been helping my parents unpack the kitchen, until, more out of an urge to get away from them than any irresistible desire to settle into our new home, I had firmly announced I was ready to tackle my room. Sitting amid the brown cardboard boxes stacked like building blocks, I considered how soul crushing it was to see all of my earthly belongings packed up and labeled "Annie's Things." It was the end of the world as I knew it, and all I had to console myself were relics of my past life—pictures and ticket stubs, old notes, and a "care package" Jamie, my best friend, had sent with me, with the insistence that it should be opened only when I *really*, *really* needed it. I figured now was as good a time as any and fished the shoe box from its bed of packing peanuts.

A knock at the door startled me. When I didn't answer immediately, it creaked open to reveal my mother. The stifling heat was bothering her, too, I could tell. Her hair was pulled back in a loose bun, and sweat stains had appeared under the arms of her orange T-shirt. With the air-conditioning on the fritz, we'd had to use knives to pry open the windows, most of which were painted shut, to avoid suffocation. Not that this was much help with the humidity, through which we could have breaststroked. And the cherry on top: we were evidently below the "gnat line," where there were more bugs than humans.

"Are you still moping?" my mom asked from the doorway.

"I prefer 'mourning,'" I answered, running my hand over the lid of the shoe box, which Jamie had decoupaged with photos and magazine clippings. "And yes."

Crossing the room to plant herself on my quilted bedspread (entirely too hot, I'd already realized, for the Seventh Circle of Hell in which we now lived), my mom sighed. I could feel her watching me, but I refused to return her gaze.

"Haven't you ever wished you could have a fresh start?" she pleaded. "This is a chance to reinvent yourself!"

"I've spent seventeen years inventing myself," I said, finally looking up from my new itchy, ugly carpet. "Why would I want to start all over again?" Wiping at the beads of sweat collecting on my upper lip, I stared at her and fought the building pressure of tears. An all-too-familiar feeling these days.

She didn't have an answer. And, all joking aside, I didn't want a fresh start. I wanted Connecticut and Deerwood Academy and Jamie. A framed picture of us stared up at me from her package. It was from Halloween, the year we'd dressed as ketchup and mustard. Our skinny legs stuck out from painted foam-board costumes as we grinned at the camera. Jamie was making the peace sign, her middle and forefinger spread into a triumphant V.

Under different circumstances, the photo would have made me smile. Now it made me feel entirely lost. Lost and adrift. Which, if you were to ask Jamie, were two feelings I valiantly opposed on a general basis. I was *not* a girl who liked change. I had lived in the same house for thirteen years, from the age of four. I'd had the same best friend since third grade and the same poster above my bed since roughly the same era. I even hated getting a haircut. Adaptation was not on my agenda.

"Well," my mother sighed again as she stood to leave, "I just wanted to remind you that we have dinner at the country club with your grandparents at six."

I stifled a groan. I hadn't seen my grandparents since I was ten, when Camp Chinakwa and field hockey clinics started to replace my annual summer visit to Gram and Pawpaw MacRae's. But I still vividly remembered my days at Belmont, the creaky, old plantation house where my father was raised. The house was magical; unfortunately, the company was not. Gram was always too busy to play (besides the fact I'd never been convinced she actually *liked* children), which left me with the twin terrors, Virginia and Charlotte, or Roberta, Gram's housekeeper, who didn't talk much but let me snap green beans on Belmont's sagging front porch.

It wasn't all bad. I remembered nights of spotlight tag and chasing lightning bugs around mammoth magnolias. And the sour, metallic smell the bugs gave off if you kept them in a jar too long or forgot to poke airholes. One summer I'd convinced Virginia and Charlotte that the house was haunted by the ghosts of slaves. Of course they'd told their mother, Aunt Nonny, who'd chased me around the yard with a switch from the weeping willow, only causing me to laugh harder.

Yet despite those moments, I always came away from my visits at Belmont with the sinking feeling that there was an essential disconnect between who I was and who Gram thought I should be. The older I'd gotten, the more interest she had taken in me, but it was interest I could have done without. One summer—my last at Belmont coincidentally—Gram had driven me to Beaufort's fanciest department store and told me I could pick out any dress I wanted. After staring at the rows and rows of pink smocking and lavender ruffles, I had opted instead for a pair of jean overalls because Jamie owned ones just like them. Gram had gotten me a dress—with ruffles—anyway.

Since that fateful summer, my relationship with my grandparents had been reduced to biannual monetary installments at Christmas and birthdays. Without fail, twice a year, I could expect a big, fat check, along with a demitasse spoon on my birthday. (My mother had to explain to me that the tiny silver spoons weren't for babies, but for fancy tea. I didn't think I'd ever use them, but as long as they were accompanied by that check, I'd take them.) I could also count on the mandatory thank-you notes my father made me write—the only time I ever used the monogrammed stationery Gram had given me when I turned thirteen.

"And you might want to wear a dress," my mother said now, flooding me with the same panicky feeling I'd experienced seven years ago in the department store.

"No way," I insisted. "That's ridiculous. I'm not dressing up for Gram and a bunch of her snobby old friends at 'the Club'!"

Turning, her hands on her hips, my mom assumed her irritated look. "I'm not asking you to get dressed up, Annie. Why don't you just wear that green sundress? The one with the big flowers."

I glanced around the bare, white room, at all the boxes still to be unpacked and the skeletal hangers in the empty closet. "Maybe. If I can find it," I granted, which roughly translated into "fat chance."

"Thank you," she said before disappearing down the hall. Two seconds later she poked her head back in the room. "Annie," she said softly this time, "I really hope you can try to be happy here."

I looked at her but didn't answer. I had really *hoped* they'd wait until after I'd graduated to move. But, as I was quickly learning, you don't always get what you want.

The Debutante *is available now
wherever books are sold.*